MW01611043

JUSTICE FOR AMBER (POLICE AND FIRE: OPERATION ALPHA)

SEEKING JUSTICE #1

JULIA BRIGHT

Dear Readers,

Welcome to the Police and Fire: Operation Alpha Fan-Fiction world!

If you are new to this amazing world, in a nutshell the author wrote a story using one or more of my characters in it. Sometimes that character has a major role in the story, and other times they are only mentioned briefly. This is perfectly legal and allowable because they are going through Aces Press to publish the story.

This book is entirely the work of the author who wrote it. While I might have assisted with brainstorming and other ideas about which of my characters to use, I didn't have any part in the process or writing or editing the story.

I'm proud and excited that so many authors loved my characters enough that they wanted to write them into their own story. Thank you for supporting them, and me!

READ ON!
Xoxo
Susan Stoker

CHAPTER 1

AMBER MILLNER WAITED for the blinking light on her computer to go dark. People thought she was ridiculous with her computer and device security, but they didn't know the projects she worked on. Working in private sector she figured she would never have the opportunity to work on national security, but then she'd developed a new way to parse data, changing the playing field for sorting the trillions of bits on the internet. The breakthrough had made her a name in certain circles.

Of course even with recognition, it didn't mean work for her wasn't grueling. She stayed late in the evening and came in early. Everyone had already left, going home to their lives, but she didn't have much of one to go home to.

She used her pass card to call the elevator, just another level of security because of her contracts. She would have used the stairs, but with the sensitive material she was working on, the stairs were only accessible in an emergency.

On the first floor she found two security guards standing around. It had to be boring working here. They were in a fenced in facility with a gate and a guard allowing access to that gate. There was no chance a random person would wander in to the building.

Amber waved to the guards as she stepped outside, knowing another guard would be waiting in his truck to escort her to her car. Again, way too much security for a regular office building.

Outside the truck pulled up beside her. "Good evening, Miss Millner."

"Hello Danny, how are you?"

"I'm good. So I have to ask, would you like a ride to your car?"

She chuckled and shook her head. "You know what I'm going to say."

He shrugged. "I know. Company protocol. So I'll slowly follow beside you like a mom driving beside her second grader who demands to walk home from school."

Amber let out a bark of laughter and shook her head as she kept walking. She'd parked on the edge of the lot which was far enough out so she registered some steps for the day. Since most of her day was spent sitting at her desk going over code, she had to walk at some point or the extra padding on her hips would go from being extra to being too much. She'd threatened her boss with the idea of getting a standup desk so she could put a treadmill under it and walk while she worked. He'd rolled his eyes and said no, telling her he didn't want to risk her falling.

When he'd said that, she'd almost thrown a fit. So she did one half marathon and ended up falling at the end. She'd been exhausted when she'd fallen and skinned her knee. She really wasn't that much of a klutz. She'd let the request go, realizing her boss wasn't going to budge. Instead, she started parking far out whenever she could.

She clicked her key fob when she was about fifteen feet away from her car. The chirp echoed off the cinderblock fence. Danny was still beside her and had turned up the music on his radio, pretending to dance in his car as he drove. She laughed at his antics, thinking the man was probably bored at this job.

Late nights had become the norm for her in the

last two months as she finished this project. Few people were out here in the evenings and Danny probably had little to do at night. She wished she didn't have to stay so late, but the demands on her were huge. She needed a break and was happy the program she was working on would be finished soon. After she turned in the project, she could get away from it all for at least a little while.

She waved to Danny before she opened her car door and slid in. The purr of the engine was oddly satisfying. She wasn't really into cars, not like some of the guys who worked here, but the Audi was her baby. Amber popped the car into gear and rolled forward about two feet when she heard a noise she didn't recognize. Then it sounded again and the glass on her rear passenger side shattered.

"Oh shit!"

The scream she let loose was almost as loud as the next shot that shattered her front windshield. Luckily she'd already made the decision to duck and had moved to a crouched position seconds before the window exploded. Her car rolled forward and she wasn't sure if she should put it in park or keep driving. Another bullet sailed into her car and she screamed again.

If she didn't get out of here, she'd end up dead.

The person shooting couldn't get closer because of the tall, cinderblock fence surrounding the property, but they were close enough to do damage.

The sharp piercing wail of a siren filled the air, giving her some peace of mind. She still didn't sit up to look. Fear made her muscles shake. Her legs were weak and her stomach rolled. She thought she might throw up. Was Danny okay?

The sirens grew closer, echoing in her head. This was going to cause all sorts of hell. With a shaky hand she pulled out her phone, nearly screaming when it vibrated. She dropped the device but picked it up quick, swiping her finger over the screen to answer.

"Hello?" She could hear the fear in her own voice and hated it.

"Amber, it's Mitch, you okay?"

"Yes, sir." Her boss had already heard. Of course he had. This would go up the chain of command fast. When your top engineer on a government computer security project was shot at in the parking lot at work, that tended to freak people out.

"I hear the sirens in the background. I'm sending in lawyers and I'll be there soon. I believe someone from the FBI will be there shortly, and a few military men will show up. Don't tell anyone what you're working on, got it? Not one person."

"Yes, sir."

She sighed, knowing this would get mired in BS so fast it would stink before the sun came up. This would be another sleepless night. There wasn't any way she'd be set loose anytime soon. Hell, she would probably be questioned for hours.

After a moment with no more shots she sat up and glanced around. Danny's truck had slammed into a light pole. She closed her eyes and whimpered. He was probably dead. There was no way this was a coincidence. Someone had targeted her, which meant she wouldn't be allowed to go home. The last thing she wanted was to be placed in protective custody, but this project was too important to screw it up. Worse, this meant someone knew what she was working on.

CHAPTER 2

THE LAST THING Cody wanted to do after a long flight and an even longer day was sit through an investigation into a shooting. He and Cruz Livingston were pulling into the parking lot of a top-rated Mexican food restaurant when the call came in. He didn't complain though he'd spent all day looking forward to getting some authentic Tex-Mex that wasn't watered down like it was in the north. This was the reason he'd moved from the Seattle FBI office to San Antonio. He'd get the good food later, and he'd be able to sleep tonight at some point once they were done on the scene.

Heck, he was used to long days and even longer nights from his stint in the Marines. He could deal with an empty belly and a tired brain for a few hours. Besides, tonight was another shit motel that would probably be louder than the one he'd stayed at the night before. His apartment wasn't ready yet and wouldn't be until tomorrow. His furniture wouldn't arrive for two more days. Basically he was stuck sleeping in crap motels until his place became available.

"You ready to get your hands dirty?" Cruz asked.

"Yes, sir."

"Dammit, Cody, don't sir me."

Cody threw back his head and laughed. "Well you are my senior since you're so much older than I am."

"Punk ass kid, that's what you've always been." They both laughed at Cruz's words.

Back when Cruz was in high school and Cody was just in seventh grade, their school had done a mentorship program. It had been the best thing for Cody since he'd been paired with Cruz. After Cruz graduated, they'd kept up with each other mainly because Cruz had written at first, but then Cody had graduated too and gone straight into the Marines, giving him some maturity he'd been lacking before. Every week he made sure to send a note to Cruz, to check in with him. They'd gone from handwritten letters to emailing. They celebrated each other's wins and Cruz helped Cody dig out from under the weight of depression when he lost his best buddy in war. When Cody had left the Marines and applied to the FBI once he finished his college work, Cruz had been more than happy to help him navigate the waters and he'd been grateful for every single piece of advice Cruz had given. Then Cruz's world had fallen apart and Cody had been there just to talk when he needed, and to play video games when he was all talked out. They were friends, and he was excited to be living so close now.

This promotion was big, well big for him. He'd packed up everything in Seattle because the brass had wanted him in San Antonio where gang warfare was hotter and the stakes were higher. There was an element of organized crime which was what Cody had specialized in during his graduate work. Now he'd been given a position where he could shine. The more he thought about it, the more he figured Cruz had put in a good word for him with the field office in San Antonio.

Cruz parked at the curb about a quarter mile away. It looked like every variation of police and law enforcement had shown up for this party. They huffed it to the perimeter tape, ducking under as they flashed their credentials. By some miracle, the press hadn't caught wind of this yet, which made their jobs easier.

"Cruz," someone called out. "We're over here."

"Hey, you get to meet the guys. Well some of them at least." Cruz headed over to three men standing close together. Cody had an idea who they were. Cruz had a good set of friends in San Antonio. They were like siblings to him. They worked for different departments in the law enforcement and first responder fields but they all fit each other from what Cruz said.

"Everyone, this is Cody. He's been a friend since I was in high school and he was what, a toddler?" Cruz's lips twitched up and he patted Cody on the shoulder.

The sense of happiness grew. Moving to San Antonio had been a huge chance, but with Cruz here, he had high hopes for his future. "Funny, Cruz, I was twelve."

"Hey, I'm Quint," the guy to his left that was about his same height with dark wavy hair stuck out his hand for a shake. "I work for SAPD."

Cody nodded and the brown-haired guy next to Quint piped up.

"I'm Dax. I'm a Texas Ranger if you couldn't tell from the hat."

"The hat is a nice touch," Cody said.

Dax chuckled. "It's a Texas thing. You'll get used to it. Where are you from?"

"Just moved here from Seattle. Actually my plane landed and Cruz picked me up at the airport promising me great food and a good time. Instead, he decided to bring me here."

"Sounds about right for Cruz," Dax joked.

The man he hadn't met, also with dark hair and even darker eyes, reached out to shake his hand. "I'm Wes. I'm also a Texas Ranger."

Cody shook his offered hand, understanding why Cruz liked this group of guys. "The hat clued me in."

"So what do we have?" Cruz asked.

"The shooter was on that building from what we can surmise. The crime scene unit is up there now," Quint said.

"Have they found casings?" Cody asked.

"Not that we've heard," Dax said, "But that's really the only place the shots could have come from."

Cruz pointed to the lot and waved his hand. "Want to walk us through the scene?"

"Sure thing," Quint said.

Dax and Wes waved as they stepped away and headed to the perimeter tape and he presumed to their cars. There were a lot of law men here right now and he guessed with the FBI on the case the Texas Rangers were stepping back.

Cody followed Quint and Cruz over to a car with the windows blown out. It was a black Audi S5. A beautiful car before being shot up. It was also above his current pay grade, but something he could see himself owning in the future if he wasn't trying to blend in.

"This belongs to Amber Millner. She was in the car at the time of the shooting but wasn't shot. Lucky woman," Quint said.

Cody turned and stared the direction Quint pointed. She wasn't hard to see. Her fiery red hair and pale skin made her hard to miss. The draw of attraction built as he stared at her. When she stomped her foot and lifted her hand, her finger waving in some big guy's face, Cody's balls tightened. He chuckled, thinking he'd love to hear what she was saying. It had to be good if the scowl on the guy's face was any indication.

"She's a firecracker," Quint said. "Under what I would call heavy fire for a civilian and yet she exited her car with an attitude bigger than the ones the Texas Rangers sport."

"Wow," Cruz said. "You know Dax will hear you say that shit eventually."

"It's good for him to hear it from me." Quint chuckled before turning to the truck and sobering. "This man wasn't as lucky, but he wasn't totally unlucky because he's alive. He was hit in the shoulder and is in surgery. They think he'll live."

"Is there a but with that?" Cody asked.

"The bullet ripped through him. He's going to have issues. Getting shot isn't fun, and this guy was hit pretty hard."

"Any clue what the motive was?" Cody glanced around, knowing they couldn't have come up with anything yet.

"No clue. We're guessing the woman was the target," Quint said.

Cody turned back to look at her, taking in her red flowing hair and sexy curves. Maybe it was the exhaustion he felt, or something else, but his desire hit hard. He wanted to trace her curves with his tongue and hold her close. He swallowed over his lust and pushed it away. Now wasn't the time to be thinking about curves and other stuff like that when he had an investigation to concentrate on.

"Want to talk to her?" Cruz asked.

Cody blew out a slow breath, fighting the urges

flowing through him. "Sure, we'll need to bring her in."

"Why were you two called in on this?" Quint asked.

"Favor to someone," Cruz said. "This place does some sort of national security programs. I'm not sure, but we were told to get over here, so here we are."

Cody's shoulders stiffened as they made their way over to the woman. She was alluring, no question. He needed to keep his defenses up. Cruz seemed relaxed, but Cody doubted Cruz was forcing desire to quell. He had Mickey at home and was head over heels in love with her. Cody hadn't met her yet but had talked on the phone to her a few times. He liked her. Honestly, Cruz's great relationship with Mickey made him jealous, but he didn't want to settle. He'd seen the damage that had done to Cruz.

"How about you do the talking?" Cruz asked as they approached.

He was in earshot of her and could hear the words she was saying.

"Well you can just tell your superiors I'm not being bullied into staying at some dump motel. I have work I have to get done," the woman shouted at the guy who appeared to be a high-ranking police officer. If Cody was right, the man was a captain.

"Ma'am, I can assure you we won't—"

"You'll do more than assure me," she stated, her voice harsh. "This is important."

"Excuse me," Cody interrupted.

The woman spun, anger flashing in her eyes, sending him a warning. His skin tingled as excitement filled him. There was enough light from the portable spotlights the cops had moved in he could see her eyes were green and she had a smattering of freckles on her face. His balls tightened and he had to force the lust down.

"Who are you and why are you here?" she barked.

Cody's lips twitched up and he noticed how her shoulders straightened. She was going to bust his balls and he looked forward to trying to please her.

"I'm Agent Cody Whittaker from the FBI, this is Agent Cruz Livingston."

"Great." She threw up her hands and rolled her eyes. "The Feds are here. I guess you think the day is saved now."

Oh yeah, she was a firecracker. The urge to smooth his fingers over her forehead, wiping away the worry hit, but he kept his hands at his side.

"I'm not going into some secret protection shit you guys love to do. I have work that has to be done."

"Yes, ma'am, Mrs. Millner."

"It's miss not missus. I'm not married. Not like that's anyone else's business. If I were—" Amber's phone rang cutting her off. She whipped it out, answering on the second ring. "Yes... Yes... No, the FBI is here."

He watched her lips turn down in a deeper frown. What was going on in her mind? He'd met victims of shootings and they usually were in shock after something so traumatic. Did she have military training?

"Which one of you two will be watching me tonight?" she barked out, her eyes going from Cody to Cruz.

"Now then Miss Millner, the San Antonio Police—"

"No, the FBI. That's what my boss told me. He's stuck in traffic, but he said the FBI is taking over my protection."

"We can take you to a safe house tonight," the San Antonio police captain.

"No, not a safe house," Amber barked.

"Ma'am," the captain said. "You do understand that we need—"

"No, it's you who don't understand. I'm not staying in a safe house, being locked away from life. I'm not giving up my freedom."

For just a moment Cody wanted to clap, but his better senses took over and he squared his shoulders, ready to go up against this woman to ensure her safety.

"Miss Millner," Cruz said. "We can arrange for a hotel and have an agent in a connecting room."

"No, a suite, that way there is only one door to come through. It will be Agent Whittaker with me, right?"

"I think it would be best if another agent, stayed in the room with you," Cody said.

"No," Amber spit out. "I don't want just anyone staying in the room with me." She pointed at him and her lips thinned. "Him, I want him."

"I don't think—"

She lifted her hand, slicing it sharply through the air. "I don't care what you think. It's Whittaker who is staying with me."

"Cody?" Cruz lifted his eye brows, asking if the plan was okay.

He should say no. He was exhausted for one thing. Second, his desire where she was concerned was off the charts. He opened his mouth, but then he looked at Amber and his heart squeezed. She'd been acting like nothing bothered her, but he saw the cracks starting to form.

"Fine," Cody said, agreeing to stay with her.

"This is unusual," Cruz said. "Cody will sleep on the couch. We'll put you up in an approved hotel in a suite where we'll have a guard set up outside—"

"SAPD can handle that," the captain said.

Cruz nodded. "Okay, so Cody will be in the den. If anyone comes into the room, he'll stop them."

Cody had doubts about his ability to wake up, but this woman was insistent and she probably wasn't actually in danger of anyone finding them. They were in more danger standing out here.

"We could probably find someone who would be a better choice," Cody warned, trying to get out of the gig now that he'd agreed.

Amber turned to him and raised one eyebrow as her lips turned down. "Are you not good at your job?"

He huffed out a breath. "I've been awake too long to say awake the whole night."

"I'm fine with taking that risk, what I'm not fine with is sleeping in a room with a total stranger."

He wanted to point out that they were total strangers, but she needed some sort of protection.

He'd do it tonight, but by tomorrow they would have someone else take over. Spending too much time with her might end up being hazardous to his health.

He gave a sharp nod. "Okay, if you insist."

"I do." Amber stared up at him, her eyes crinkled, and her lips thinned. "I drink good coffee. Do they have a coffee shop in the lobby?"

Cruz piped up. "Yes, ma'am. I'll make sure you have some good java in the morning."

Amber turned to Cruz. "Can we stop by my place for clothes?"

Cruz shook his head. "No ma'am. If they were targeting you, we have to assume they are watching where you live. I can't take that chance tonight. We'll have someone check out your place in the morning and will know more. You'll just have to stick with Cody for now."

"Tomorrow, after we go through the interview process at the FBI office, I'll drive you to work," Cody stated. "Someone will pick you up in the evening."

"What's to prevent them from shooting me in your car?" Amber asked.

This woman was smart. Nothing really would prevent someone from following them and shooting at them. Since they had no clue who was trying to take her out, they had no idea how to protect her other than just general ideas they would use for anyone.

"I'll arrange for a special car," Cody said.

She lifted an eyebrow and tilted her head so she was looking down her nose at him though he was taller than her by a good five inches. "Special? How special?"

"Super special," he said with a smile.

She rolled her eyes and he almost laughed. Someone stepped close who obviously knew Miss Millner and she turned to talk to him. Cruz stepped away to arrange for a hotel while he stood there staring at the woman with red hair, thinking spending time with her was a mistake.

"You don't have to do this tonight. We can get someone else to come in," Cruz said, as he came back.

"Eh, it's fine. I'm good with this arrangement and besides, it's only for one, maybe two nights until we figure out what protection she actually needs."

Cruz's lips twisted in a grimace. "It could be longer."

"Then I'll get backup. Listen, this is why I moved here. We don't know if this is related to terrorism or organized crime, or if by chance it was a one-off thing. Someone needs to stay with this woman and work out if this is something deeper than some random shooting done by some idiot with a gun. If we don't get close enough to figure out what was going on in her life, we won't know where the threat is coming from. And who knows, by tomorrow we might find it was just some random jerk who had a gun and wanted to use it."

Amber had caught the last of what the agent had said and wanted to tell him he was full of shit, but she was tired, her boss was here, and she really wanted a drink and bed, though she would probably just fall into bed.

"Are you ready?" she asked the FBI agents.

"Yes, ma'am. I'm ready to go," Cody said.

"I don't remember which one you are, Cruz or Cody?"

"I'm Cody."

"Sweet, now let's go. I'm exhausted and need a drink." She took off, unsure exactly where they were going but a hand on her arm stopped her.

"Hold up there, ma'am," Cody's deep voice rumbled.

Heat raced up her shoulder to her neck and then down her spine. She figured her cheeks were red with blush based on how hot she felt. Stupid pale, reactive skin. The man had her on edge already and his touch sent her into overdrive. His lips were thin but dark and his eyes seemed to see everything. She liked the way they lingered on her, like a warm blanket on a cold winter night. A man like that made her want to move north so she would have to cuddle with him to stay warm.

Heck, the second she'd seen him she'd wanted to remove his suit jacket and see what was hiding under those layers of clothes. The thought of licking down his chest, tracing his abs had made her knees weak.

She needed to take a break from work and have some fun, but that wouldn't happen until her project was completed.

Not wanting this man to know he affected her, she didn't look at him, instead she waited until he stepped close and moved to stand in front of her.

"Are we not ready to leave?" She cringed because she sounded like a bitch and she really didn't want to, but this man was so intense, beautiful, and intriguing. If she could reach up and touch his face, maybe see if he was real, she could get past this instant infatuation, but they weren't at a bar and this wasn't a pickup club.

His shoulders stiffened. "I need Agent Livingston to drop us off."

She huffed out a breath, not wanting this guy to know he made her hot all over. Sleeping near him would be difficult. She'd insisted it be him because when he'd stepped close, something calmed inside her. She felt protected just having him near.

It had been too long since she'd dated anyone, which meant it had been even longer since the last time she'd had sex. Solving the issue by hooking up with some random dude wasn't her way, but honestly this hot FBI agent with dark eyes, a good dusting of stubble, a sexy smile, and a rocking body from what she could tell was under his suit had her turned on so much she would take anyone...maybe not anyone, but she wanted to get laid so badly.

She turned to the other FBI Agent and forced a smile. "Agent Livingston, can we go now? I'm tired and need a drink."

"Yes, ma'am," Cruz drawled like a true Texan, exaggerating every word. "We aim to serve."

She rolled her eyes. "That's not the FBI motto is it?"

"No ma'am," Cody said as they headed out to Cruz's waiting car. He opened the door for her and paused until she was inside the car before he shut it and met Cruz's gaze. Cruz lifted his eyebrows and Cody shot him a smile. He didn't care how difficult this woman appeared, he wanted nothing more than to spend time with her, but he sure as hell wasn't going to let on to Cruz how much he wanted to be near Miss Millner.

Too many months had passed since the last time he'd been with a woman in anything other than a professional capacity, and while there were good looking women who worked for the FBI, he'd decided a long time ago he would never mix business with pleasure. No way, no how would he allow himself to date another person who worked for the FBI, and since he'd been working overtime to get noticed, he'd let that part of his life slip.

"So what is the motto?" Amber asked as he clicked his seatbelt closed.

"Don't screw up," Cody replied without hesitation.

Cruz fought to keep a straight face and Amber stayed silent. The traffic decreased as they drove. He noticed Cruz checking the mirrors for people following them. They made a few unnecessary turns on their way to the hotel, throwing off any tails. From what he could see, they weren't being followed.

The FBI had arranged for the room, so it wasn't under his name or Amber's. The San Antonio Police stationed a guy at the hotel to keep an eye out until the FBI could arrange something more permanent.

Cody stepped into the room first and opened the bathroom door, checking in the shower before heading to the bedroom to look under the bed, in the closet, and behind the door. Maybe it was unnecessary, but it was habit. He closed the curtains in the bedroom before meeting Amber in the main room.

"I'll be on the couch. If you need anything, just ask. Don't open the curtains, even if you think you need to. There isn't anything out there to see anyway." He moved to the curtain in the main room and pulled it closed.

"I hate this," Amber said, her voice so soft he had to strain to hear her speak.

He turned, staring at her for a moment before pushing away the desire she inspired. "We all do. Every single one of us hates when someone gets shot. Now we just have to figure out why you were being shot at, and if it was really you they were shooting at."

Amber cocked her head to the side. "What does that mean? Who else would they have been shooting at?"

"It could have been random. Danny was actually hit, so it could have been him."

"He was, but my car was shredded. My poor car. I loved that freaking car." Her lips thinned and her brows bunched.

He wasn't used to being shot at, but he'd gotten to the point it didn't freak him out so much while he was in the military. For a civilian to be shot at was a big deal. She seemed very calm for the situation.

"I'm sorry. It sucks, but we won't dismiss any possibility until we investigate it. Once Danny is out of surgery, we'll question him. We'll make sure he doesn't have any big gambling debts."

"Is that what you think this is?" Her nose wrinkled. "Some retribution for gambling?"

Cody hit her with a deadpan stare, forcing his anger to stay down. He was exhausted and not ready to deal with work BS, but he'd gladly taken on the task of staying at this hotel because they both needed a place to sleep and crimes like this one were exactly why he'd come here. Frustration mixed with hunger and exhaustion, leaving him vulnerable to saying or doing something stupid. He took a calming breath before he answered.

"No, not really, but I'm not lazy, and the last

thing I would ever do is overlook something because it seems ridiculous."

Amber nodded then her lips thinned. "So is Danny going to be okay?"

He'd received a text but that was almost an hour ago. "I don't know. They haven't updated me recently. The last update said he would make it. Getting shot is rough." A memory of his buddy surfaced; his smile cut short because of a bullet. He shuddered, forcing the image away.

Luckily Amber had closed her eyes as she shook her head. "I hope he is okay. I'm going to get some sleep."

"I'm ordering food for delivery, would you like anything?"

"No, I just need to pass out and forget what happened."

He felt for her. He would find a psychologist for her to talk to. The FBI had victims support advocates. In Seattle he knew who to call, down here he'd have to rely on Cruz to help him out.

"Sure, get some sleep. I'll be out here if you need anything."

Amber disappeared into the bedroom and he grabbed his computer from his bag and opened it so he could order takeout. He called down to the cop playing guard duty and told him to expect a delivery. Cody had ordered the guy a burger and fries too and made sure the officer knew to take it when the food arrived.

He checked email while he waited. The bedroom door cracked open and Amber stepped out and slipped into the bathroom without a word.

His email had lit up in the last hour and he spent time going through the notes about the case and information about San Antonio. He replied to a few emails from FBI friends in Seattle. Before he knew it, the food was here. The first bite was like balm to his soul. He'd been so hungry he'd almost grown used to the pain in his belly.

With the food consumed he closed his eyes and then flashed them open, realizing he needed to brush his teeth before he turned in for the night.

It was a little odd spending the night in the same room as a complete stranger. He'd done it before. Usually he didn't sleep, but this was so last minute, and they had the police downstairs he felt he could get some rest, though he wouldn't slip into deep sleep.

He needed to gain some focus on this case. Amber was smoking hot, but she was now under FBI protection which meant he couldn't touch her.

Whoever had tried to kill her had missed, which made him wonder if it was a general warning, or if someone had acted hastily, thinking they could get the job done without really contemplating all the issues surrounding trying to kill someone. This was going to be a tough week and stepping into a case so soon after moving wasn't going to make it any easier for him.

CHAPTER 3

AMBER JOLTED AWAKE, her heart hammering and her hands shaking. She wasn't in her own bed and it took a moment to figure out where she was. Then it all came back, the gun shots, the police, the FBI agents, Danny being shot. Tears sprang to her eyes and she swiped at them, angry someone had targeted her. It had to be her work.

Her mind twisted to Danny. The guy was nice, but what if he'd racked up gambling debt. She didn't want to think badly of him, but like the FBI agent had said, it could be anything. There even could have been some random dude up on the other building just having fun by shooting at people. The idea was farfetched, but people were crazy.

Amber had taken off her clothes before

stretching out. She grabbed her shirt and tugged it over her head, catching a glimpse of herself in the mirror. She looked like shit. She tugged on her pants, wanting to go home and take a long shower. That wasn't going to happen right now. She steeled her shoulders and stepped out into the main room. Soft snores that made her stomach twist came from Agent Whittaker. For a second she thought about stepping close to watch him sleep, but the need to pee won out.

Whittaker was hot, and he was asleep in her room. The thought of watching him made her throat tighten. She imagined running her hand over his shoulders and down his torso, sliding her fingers under the edge of his waistband, dipping lower until —She grunted, forcing the lust driven thoughts away.

After she finished in the bathroom, she stepped into the main room and Cody sat up, his Glock in his hand.

"What?" He blinked at her twice then shook his head as he lowered his gun. "Oh, it's you."

Guilt from her imaginations filled her. "Yes, it's me." Her words were stiff and once again she sounded like a bitch. Sometimes she hated that she had to act so bitchy just to get people to listen. Sure, she was a red headed short girl with big hips and boobs. For some stupid reason that automatically made people think she was stupid. Living through years of being ignored, she'd grown a tough shell and an attitude to force people to pay attention to her. If she didn't put up with their bullshit and called them on their crap, they listened to her. She guessed she could have chosen to just be some guy's arm candy, but she wanted more for her life. Right now, she wanted to finish this program at work.

Cody grunted and wiped his face before he leaned forward and stood. "I need coffee. I'll be a better person once I have something to help me wake up. It's early for me."

"It's five thirty."

Cody wiped at his face again and groaned. "I just moved from Seattle."

She felt bad automatically. "Oh, I guess it is early there," Amber stepped over to the small kitchenette where a coffee maker was located. "I need coffee, too."

"Same." Cody groaned as he stood. "I just said that, didn't I?"

She moaned. "This stuff is a joke."

"Let me use the restroom and we'll go find something good."

She turned and stared at him. "You wore your clothes to sleep in?"

He glanced down at his wrinkled shirt, not even bothering to smooth it out. "I did."

"I'm shocked. I couldn't sleep in my clothes."

Cody pushed away her comment and went to the bathroom, ignoring the half wood in his pants. She didn't have any clue her words had turned him on. Heck, it wasn't only her words but her attitude too. She wasn't shaking and crying because someone had shot at her, instead she was ready to raise hell. He appreciated that about her.

He's set his Glock down on the counter while he used the restroom. After he brushed his teeth, he splashed water on his face and used a towel to dry. He stared at himself in the mirror, thinking he looked terrible. His clothes were awful, his stubble was too long to be considered stubble, and there were dark rings around his eyes. He'd stayed up too late and woke too early. The move was catching up to him and exhaustion was tugging him down. His phone rang and he answered.

"Agent Whittaker here."

"Cody, it's Cruz. How is she?"

He stared at the bathroom door, knowing she could hear everything he said. "Good."

"Are you ready for coffee?" Cruz asked.

"Yes."

"Excellent. I'm coming to get you two and we'll go over to HQ and have a meeting. We start early here."

"Oh God, I look like crap."

"Well, you have your suitcase, I suggest you change."

Cody rolled his eyes. "Sure thing."

He grabbed his gun and opened the bathroom door. When he stepped into the main room, Amber looked ready to leave. "I need to change and shave."

"We have time?" she asked. "Wasn't that someone coming to pick us up?"

He nodded. "Yes, it was, but it will only take me a moment."

Amber rolled her eyes and he couldn't tell if she was pissed he was taking the time to change, or if she was just making a general silent statement about everything. This woman didn't seem like the type to put up with annoyances.

He picked up his suitcase and took it into the bathroom along with his Glock which he never lost track of. It was an extension of his body. He either wore his piece or had it locked in his storage case. He knew some guys had no issue setting their guns down, trusting others to leave them alone, but not him. He didn't want his gun to ever wind up in the wrong hands.

He washed quickly in the shower, then shaved his stubble, wishing for once the FBI would accept him with a few days growth. When he'd been in the Marines, he'd been on a detail that allowed him to look scruffy. He'd relished his long hair and beard. Of course in the FBI they liked his hair longer then Marine-issue jarhead cuts, but it was still short compared to where he'd like it.

Once he was dressed, his gun in his holster, he opened the door to find Amber sitting on a chair with her computer open. She shut the lid fast, looking guilty.

He paused, warnings going off in his head. Curiosity filled him but he covered it and stepped into the room, ignoring the fact she still seemed guilt-ridden.

"Cruz will be here soon. We'll get coffee and head to the office."

"I need to go to work," Amber said.

"I'm sure you do. We'll figure out at the office what needs to be done, and how we're going to handle it."

"You mean me?"

She hit him with a level stare. He wished he could deny what he meant, but she had caught on to him. They had to decide what to do with her. For some reason, he didn't think this was a random shooting. Her guilty attitude this morning told him it was so much deeper than someone shooting at her.

Amber knew it was risky pulling out her computer with Cody in the same room. She never allowed anyone to see what she was actually working on. Not that her company allowed her access to the code outside of work, but she didn't need the code in front of her to remember the sections well enough to write notes she could use later to fix problems.

Once finished, the program would be the best terrorist tracking software around. She'd been working with Homeland Security on this program for over a year, and they were down to the final rounds of testing. Her breakthrough on sorting data made the difference. The sheer amount of information on the internet overwhelmed most systems so it took a human to actually look at the material, but humans missed important signs. This wouldn't replace the analyst on the job, but it would augment their work, making them much more efficient. They could tie in people who were missed in their initial sweeps of information when they found a terrorist cell. It would give the guys in the field more to go on. Basically, it would make the world safer for everyone, including law enforcement.

Only because of the recent change in laws had they been allowed to consider this solution. Some people thought the program would impinge upon freedom, but it would actually reduce the number of innocent people accused of terrorism.

The key to her program's success, above the data sorting issues, was it didn't just look at one thing. It crawled through the internet, gathering IP addresses, information, key words, phrases, names, keeping track of everyone who was tagged as a potential terrorist subject and then the program sorted the information based on information law enforcement needed. Analysts could quickly gather information about a terrorist cell and not miss people who were on the fringe. It was the big behemoth to take down organized crime rings and terrorist operating in the United States.

She guessed information on her project was out. She should have known someone would sell her out. But how many people knew about the project, and who knew she was the person working on it?

Cody's phone buzzed and he pulled it from his pocket. "Cruz is here with coffee."

"Oh, thank God." She needed a good cup of java after last night.

Cody chuckled and moved to the door, his hand on his gun. Then she noticed how he visibly relaxed and popped open the door.

"Good morning, Cody, Miss Millner. It's good to see you," Cruz said as he strolled in.

"You're awfully chipper this morning," Cody said.

"I'm naturally happy now." Cruz set the cardboard coffee cup holder down on the counter and turned to her. "So, I've been chatting with a friend over at Homeland Security."

"Oh." She froze as her stomach clenched. The guy she was working with at Homeland had told her not to talk about her work. Because of this shooting, people like Cruz and Cody would know about the program. She wondered if they had the government clearance necessary to talk with them.

"So my friend at Homeland, he knows who you are," Cruz said.

Cody reached for a cup of coffee and narrowed his gaze at her. She squirmed and then blew out a breath. They were going to find out. This whole thing could blow up.

She glanced around, feeling too exposed. If it was someone at Homeland Security, it had to be one of the guys on the project she was working on. Again, the warnings about not talking to anyone came to mind. She swallowed over her fear, needing time to figure out what she could say. "We can't talk here."

"FBI office?" Cruz asked. "We can get a conference room."

"It's top secret," she said. "I probably can't speak about it unless you have high enough clearance."

"We have clearance," Cruz said.

"Are you sure?" She picked up a cup of coffee and took a sip, moaning at the flavor. "This is good."

"Thank you, and yes, we're rated for top secret clearance. I'll call my friends in Homeland Security. They'll make sure we both can be read-in on what you're working on."

Amber blew out a harsh breath. It would be nice to talk about everything with someone other than the few other people on the project.

"Grab your bag, Cody," Cruz tossed over his shoulder as he moved to the door. "It's time to head out."

Amber made sure she had her purse and computer then followed Cruz as he left the hotel room. There was a cop sitting in a chair two doors down. The guy stood and nodded as they walked past. He followed them to the elevator.

"Thank you, Officer Wilson," Cody said.

"Yes, sir. It was a pleasure."

Amber wondered if he was lying about it being a pleasure. She couldn't imagine sitting in a hall watching for nothing to happen. But then again, she'd always been about the action. Funny she would end up programing computers, but the programs she created were exciting.

They drove over to the FBI office which took almost thirty minutes. Once there, she was given another cup of coffee and whisked into a conference room. She only had to wait about ten minutes before two people in suits stepped in. Cody followed behind them. She wondered where Cruz was, but she figured he would probably be around later.

"Miss Millner, I'm Supervisory Special Agent Riley, and this is Senior Special Agent Anderson. Special Agent Whittaker will be managing your case."

Her gaze cut to Cody and she wondered why he'd left off the Special part of his title yesterday.

Cody lifted his gaze from the piece of paper he'd been studying. She had to glance away because his eyes were too beautiful and intense to look at with the other men present. If she kept staring at him, she would reveal how much she wanted him.

"Are you okay with that?" Riley asked.

"Yes, sir." She looked back to Cody, noticing he was writing something on a sheet of paper. She wished she was sitting beside him so she could try to figure out what he was writing.

"So the project you were working on," Cody said. "How close are you to deploying it?"

She swallowed, still bugged that she was talking about a top-secret project with someone she wasn't sure she could trust. It wasn't really that she didn't think she could trust him, but her work was sensitive and she'd spent months not trusting anyone. "It's very close."

"We need to figure out who wants you out of the picture. Does anyone else know about your project?"

She wasn't sure exactly how much she could say. These guys said they had clearance, but she'd sworn she wouldn't speak to anyone about her work. Her throat felt dry, her lips parched so she took a sip of coffee, which only helped a little.

"What do you know about the program I'm working on?" Her gaze moved from man to man, finally landing on Cody.

"It's an anti-terrorism tool," Agent Riley said.

She nodded, thinking they hadn't had the full impact of the program explained to them. "It's more than just your usual tool. I know we have analysts who comb through information, this takes their tasks and completes them in a fraction of the time. No other program out there can match the speed of mine."

"What if it messes up?" Cody asked.

"It could, that's why the information is still looked at by a human, but when analysts go into work in the morning, they'll be given a list of say eight men who are working together across the globe, all the chat rooms they visit, their addresses, everything questionable they've done online. The analyst checks that information and they can escalate it to a team that can take down the terrorist cell. Yes, our current analysts do a great job, but it takes time and they may miss critical information. My program will make it easier for men like you to do your job."

"Is it online yet? Like working?" Riley asked.

"Only in the background. The agents don't have access to the data real time. We've been doing quality testing. There are minor things I have to tweak before we go live to run the beta test."

Riley leaned forward; his expression serious.

"Why did you develop this? Why not someone who already works for the government?"

She narrowed her gaze at him and almost said something snarky. She held back. "Because I'm good."

Riley leaned in even more. "What does that mean?"

"It means I have a unique set of skills that not everyone else has. I can get this job done. If I worked for the US government, they wouldn't allow me to create like I do on my own. I'd have to follow certain guidelines, which is great when you're talking about what you guys do, but I don't like being constrained."

Cody took a sip of his coffee then leaned forward. "Amber, who knew you were close to finishing?"

"My contact at Homeland, my boss, and a few other people in the company, and not really anyone else. I don't discuss my work with anyone. I go home and blow off steam playing video games, but I don't really talk. I have a group I play online games with, but they all think I'm a pizza delivery girl."

"What?" Laughter spilled from Cody's mouth.

"I told them the first time I met them that I delivered pizza. It was easier than telling them the truth."

"Smart," Cody said. "I keep my job from the guys

who I play with, but I never came up with something that smart."

"So we have no real leads. No possible suspects, no one who knew you were close to being done with the job, and yet we had someone get up on a building across the street from your office and shoot with a high-powered rifle, trying to kill you," Riley said.

"How is Danny?" Amber asked.

"He's going to live. They have him sedated. We have an agent on him. Once he wakes up, he'll be able to talk, hopefully."

Cody cleared his throat, getting her attention. "We're going to need access to your bank records."

Amber nodded then things clicked. She sat up straighter and tapped the table in front of her. "Wait, you think I did this?"

Cody shook his head. "We have to clear everyone. Even Danny is a suspect."

"But Danny had no clue what I do for work. For all he knows I could be a secretary."

"I doubt he ever thought that," Cody said.

"Why?" Amber demanded.

Cody blinked at her, unsure what to say next. She drove too nice of a car, and her attitude wasn't low key. But he couldn't say that out loud.

Supervisor Riley's phone buzzed and Cody sat up straighter. He didn't want to disappoint his new command structure. He'd almost forgotten he was the new kid on the block and blurted out something silly. He didn't mean anything by his words, but Amber had impressed him and now here she was challenging him.

"I need to take care of something else," Riley said as he stood and Anderson stood with him. "Special Agent Whittaker will get the information we need and finish taking your statement."

"Yes, sir. It was nice meeting you," Amber said.

She had manners and she was smart. He would have to watch himself or risk losing his sanity. He forced away the desire and concentrated on the information they needed. He pushed a sheet of paper her way and flashed a quick smile.

"If you could, give us permission to go over your accounts," Cody asked.

"I don't like this."

"I know, but it's better if you allow us to look rather than forcing us to get a warrant." He didn't like having to pressure her into this, but it was his job. He had to get to the bottom of this and find out exactly what had gone wrong. He would make sure justice was served in this case.

Amber took the paper and wrote out information. After a moment she looked up at him and her lips were down in a frown. He moved over to sit next to her.

"I know this is a lot, but we need to catch this guy. We have no clue who is going after you or if the guy was even targeting you or it was someone else. We can't protect you if we don't know."

Amber nodded then finished writing out her passwords for her social media.

"I'm sorry," Cody whispered.

"It's okay. It's not like there is anything interesting on social media. It's mainly just stuff from high school friends and a few college buddies. I don't list my real job there. I figured it's not any of their business."

"Okay, so that's it?" Cody looked at the list of social media, seeing that really she only belonged to Facebook and Instagram.

"That's it."

"The analyst will look over these."

Amber chuckled and he lifted his eyebrows. She shook her head as she spoke. "It's just funny that my program may have been able to find this guy and stop him before he even shot me."

"That's sounding a little Minority Reportish."

She shrugged. "I get that. It's not like that, instead it looks at things that happen, like who buys what ammunition. Also these guys don't operate in a vacuum."

"I know," Cody said. "Now then, how about we head to your place and pick up some clothes for you."

"Is it safe?"

"Yes. We've had people watching your building. No one has gone in our out of your unit."

"Thank God. I want a good shower and my own clean clothes."

He reached for her bag and she tugged it closer to her body. "I can handle it."

"I'm sure you can. I'll carry it for you if you like."

"There's no need. I'm good."

He opened the door for her and led her out of the building, stopping by Cruz's desk to pick up an envelope for him. He'd been given use of an FBI car for the next two weeks. It was large and black, and totally screamed FBI. He had little doubt everyone would know what he was when he pulled up driving this car. He was thankful he had use of a car.

Amber seemed nervous and he understood. A killer could be positioned anywhere in the area just waiting to strike. Eventually protection wouldn't be provided and Amber would have to figure out a way to adjust and cope with the fact someone had shot at her and wanted her dead. He saw a therapist in her future and maybe even a move to a different city or place to work, but that may not even help.

If someone wanted Amber dead, they wouldn't stop searching for her just because she moved locations. Her life wouldn't improve until they figured out the who and why.

He pulled into the lot of her condo which was located in a high rise on the east side of the main freeway that cut through the town. He liked the area but wondered if the road noise would be too much. The building was luxurious with thick carpeting and artistic prints in the hallway. His apartment in Seattle was a shithole compared to this place. The complex he'd chosen here would also be considered way below this place's standards.

"How long have you lived here?" he asked as she keyed into her apartment.

"I bought the place two years ago. It's nice." She pushed the door open and they both stepped in.

He stalled, staring out at the city of San Antonio. "Wow, great view."

"I know, right. I love it. That's why I've stayed

here. I love watching the city when I wake up in the mornings. The sunset isn't bad either."

"Well, this place is amazing."

Amber faced him and her gaze turned serious. "Do I have time to shower and change?"

"Sure. I'll set up out here and make a few calls."

"Okay. I'll be just a few minutes."

He wanted to chuckle. If she was anything like the girlfriends he'd had in the past, those few minutes would be hours. He pulled out his phone and opened his email, checking for anything from his new boss first. This wasn't how starting a new position was supposed to go. He should be in his boss's office right now learning what was expected of him. Instead he was babysitting an apparently rich woman who intrigued him beyond just finding her killer.

He needed to quit thinking about her as some sexy siren. This wasn't the time or the place. Of course right now she was in the other room naked, taking a shower. He blew out a breath and focused on his email. As he read an email he realized he wasn't able to hear anything from the freeway below. He was amazed. This place really was nice.

He opened a note from his boss and found the man wasn't angry, instead he was happy with how

Cody had stepped in and taken care of the shooter's target. They were making progress on the case, but it was slow going. He wrote out a memo of what he'd learned and made notes for what he needed to accomplish.

He had reservations for a new hotel for the both of them this time staying in connecting rooms. Tomorrow night, he would be relieved and she would be handed off to someone else if they felt she couldn't go home. He needed to get her to talk more about her work, who had it in for her, who would want her dead. They needed to go over who knew when she would be done working and who she talked to on a daily basis. With the program she was working on, the idea that terrorist had targeted her was fairly high.

The door opened and Amber stepped out of her bedroom. She was dressed in black slacks, a black blouse, and she either had no makeup on or she knew exactly how to apply it. Her hair was braided at the back and looked very smooth. His fingers twitched at the urge to reach over and undo her braid. The thought of running his hands through her hair had his cock going hard.

He shoved away the desire. "I'd like to talk to you about your work."

She nodded and set the bag she'd been carrying in the entryway. Her movements were stiff and her eyes pinched like she was sad.

Amber said nothing as she moved to her kitchen and began making coffee. Her appliances were stainless, the cabinets dark, almost espresso in color. The place was clean, not one spoon left out, nothing open on the counters, and when she opened her pantry, it looked neat.

"So, what do you want to know?" Amber asked after pouring in water and starting the coffee maker.

"Did you normally leave at the same time each day?"

"No. This project has been kicking my butt. I'm almost done, but not quite there. I just have a few more adjustments and then I'll be able to turn in a fully complete project. Since I know I'm close, I work late. I have to get this done before our delivery date, but it has to be right. Some nights I'm there until midnight. I can't take this work home, it's too sensitive to work remote. This is a behemoth of a project. It's too important to allow anyone to install a backdoor."

"I'm still surprised someone on the government payroll didn't write this piece of software. Like aren't they afraid you'll install a backdoor?"

"Maybe, but I won't. I want domestic terrorist caught as much as you do."

"Why?"

Amber's eyes got a faraway look and pain flashed across her face. "I lost my best friend to a school shooting that could have been prevented. The guy showed all the signs, was in the chat rooms, had ordered items that my program would trigger an inquiry on."

Her words were filled with sadness. She'd had to deal with too much at a young age. He wanted to find this jerk now more than ever. He cleared his throat. "So about exiting the building, do you always park out so far?"

"Yes. I need more steps, you know, walking. I've been too busy to go to the gym. I try to get my steps in while I'm heading into work and leaving."

He wanted to tell her she was perfect as she was, that she didn't need any exercise, but it wasn't his place to say that to her. "So why didn't they shoot you when you were walking out to your car?"

"I don't know."

She closed her eyes and her lips thinned. When she opened them, he nearly lost his focus again. Her green eyes were clouded with confusion and pain.

He wanted to pull her into his arms and hold her close.

"I guess Danny's truck was between me and the shooter. He drove beside me all the way out to my car."

Cody made a note of that. "Do you usually do that?"

She nodded and a harsh chuckle escaped her lips. For a second he feared she would breakdown. "Danny does that all the time. He's funny and likes to kid around. Last night he was pretending to dance in his truck. He had music going and was doing funny moves. There isn't much that goes on out there. I mean the security is thick. There are plenty of guys in the building and on the grounds. I'm sure they are all as shocked as I am that a shooting happened. I just…I don't understand why it happened."

Amber grabbed a mug and poured a cup of coffee which she then set in front of him. She picked up another mug, this one red with a golden crown on the front—it suited her—and poured herself a cup then took a seat on a stool at the bar separating the kitchen from the den. He pulled the stool next to her out and settled on it.

"This program I've developed, it could bring down a lot of people. It could change the way we fight terrorism. It also could pick up illegal activity from people inside the government or really anywhere."

He lifted the mug, taking a long sniff before taking a sip. The black brew was rich and delicious, much better than the coffee he made at home.

"I don't know enough about the tech stuff," he said. "But I can appreciate what you are saying though I don't understand how it would be possible and why what we already have in place wouldn't work. Anyway, I hope whoever is targeting you isn't with the government."

She met his gaze and held it. A shiver skated down his back though he fought to repress it. The moment passed, and instead of the intensity holding him in place, it was his desire for her. He wondered how soft her cheek would feel under the pad of his thumb as he gently caressed her. Undeniable desire flowed through him, but work took precedence. He may want to get to know her better, to see what she tasted like and felt like in his arms, but not yet.

He sat up straight, fighting the urge to kiss her, and took another sip of coffee then stood, knowing that being in her place like this was too comfortable. He cleared this throat, trying to forget about how sexy she was and focus on the tasks that needed to be completed.

"I need to take you to work."

"Sure, let me pour this into a travel mug." Amber took a couple of sips of her coffee as she moved into the kitchen.

He lifted his mug and drank about half the coffee, deciding even her coffee was tempting. He wanted more time with her. He let his gaze travel over her legs and up to her hips, wondering how she would feel pressed up against him.

"Okay, I'm ready," Amber said as she turned.

Cody tried to act like he wasn't affected by her, but it had to be obvious. "I'll drop you at your office and check to make sure the area is secured. There will be a police officer around all day. Someone, either me or another agent will be picking you up after work. Don't leave the building."

She rolled her eyes and scoffed. "I won't. I'm not an idiot. Besides, I don't have a car now and I still have loads of work."

He winced. She was stuck at work, all because some jerk had shot up her car. "I'm sure you're not an idiot, I just want you thinking about your safety. You're used to going where you want, when you want, but this is different. Someone wants you dead and we need to make sure that doesn't happen."

Cody checked the hall before he led Amber from her residence to the elevator and down to the car. Being near her had him turned on most of the time. Her curves were sexy and she was smart. He liked how fast thinking she was and he liked her smart mouth.

On the drive in he thought about her program and what type of person it would target. If someone on the inside of the government wanted her gone, he figured she would already be dead.

He parked by the curb near the main entry for her building and walked her in, checking the office where she worked. Everything was clear and in less than a half hour he was able to leave and head to his new office in the FBI building near the outside freeway loop around San Antonio.

His stomach churned as he pulled into the parking lot two hours late. This wasn't exactly how he wanted to start his first day of work under his new boss, but at least he was late because he'd been protecting a victim. His equilibrium was off. Going from the plane to a case had thrown him, but he couldn't allow it to show. He straightened his tie as he stepped from the car. For a moment doubt surfaced, reminding him he was in over his head, but he pushed it away, instead focusing on the positives going for him. He had done well in his master's degree, and he'd performed well at work in Seattle. He could do a good job here, not only because he wanted it, but he had to do more than meet expectations to keep this job.

CHAPTER 4

CODY SPENT a few hours going through orientation and set up of his new ID along with his office. He had a desk on the far side of a bullpen with twenty other desks. His end goal was to get an actual office with a door for privacy, but that took time.

Cruz came up behind him, calling out to him before sitting in the chair beside his desk. "Agent Whittaker. Wow, same little kid I met when I was a senior in high school. It seems so long ago and yet here you are as an agent. I'm impressed. Really. It takes a lot to become an agent and you did it. It's really good to have you here. So how did last night really go?"

He liked being in the same office as Cruz. It was good to have someone who he knew was a friend.

"I'm exhausted, but I got the job done. Nothing happened, which was good."

Cruz chuckled. "That is good."

"I'm set up here, what's next on the list?"

"We need to conduct a few interviews. There've been leads called into the police, but nothing major has tweaked anyone's interest. It's just your basic list of things people call in about, you know, like neighbors people don't like, someone suspecting their husband, things like that."

"Any chance any of the tips are real?"

Cruz shook his head. "Doubtful. You know how it is, everyone wants to call in and get a piece of fame."

"Yeah, sadly I do." He stood and grabbed his jacket, pulling it on. He followed Cruz to the elevator, his mind drifting to Amber. He wanted to protect her and it was deeper than just being an agent and her needing help. He felt things for her he hadn't felt in a long time. It had to be lust mixed with exhaustion. But he knew that wasn't the only thing piquing his interest. Amber was special.

He and Cruz headed to police headquarters where they found their contact, Detective Buckalew.

"Hey Cruz, and I don't remember your name," Buckalew said as he looked Cody up and down.

"Cody Whittaker, I just moved here from Seattle."

"Well, you're in the thick of it now." The guy chuckled as he pointed to a room with a table and chairs.

"I agree," he said as he took a seat on the far side of the table in the conference room. "I came here because of the increased organized crime."

"We do it big in Texas." Detective Buckalew laughed as he sat. "So what do you think about this one?"

"So far we have nothing," Cruz said.

"So you're going to be like that," Buckalew asked.

"Don't be that way," Cruz said. "You know we can't share anything."

"I know, you expect the world from us, but you won't give." Buckalew shook his head. "If things were different."

"But they aren't. And you're happy."

Buckalew nodded. "I am, for the most part. I spoke with Quint this morning. He said you were a great guy and to not give you too much hell."

Cruz threw back his head and laughed. "Sounds about right. So what did your guys find?"

Buckalew's lips twisted into a grimace as he pulled out a file then turned on a tablet computer. "The casings were Creedmoor."

"Really?" Cruz asked.

"Yes. I'm not sure if that means the shooter was a local boy who was just having fun, a serious hunter, or someone wanting to throw us off the path. Creedmoor shells are widely available here." Buckalew met Cody's gaze and his lips thinned.

"Do you think it was a local guy?" Cody asked.

"No clue," Buckalew said. "There's so much hunting around here it's actually dangerous at times. Having this round is normal here. Hell, teenagers carry them around in the glovebox of their trucks, or they did before the world went to shit and kids had to stop carrying their hunting rifles in the gunracks of their trucks."

Cody nodded, what would happen if people still had gunracks. It would be an invitation to break into a car.

"Meaning he or she could have picked that ammunition up anywhere, even Walmart," Cruz offered.

"So were there any cameras?" Cody asked.

"There were, but the guy wore a full facemask in addition to a long sleeve shirt and gloves. We don't know what race, if it was a man or a woman, anything other than basic height which was around five nine," Buckalew said.

"The cameras, could I have access?" Cody asked.

"Sure, we'll set you up," Cruz said.

"We may need boots on the ground, going from business to business in the path this guy took to escape."

"That's the thing. We lost him in a dense set of trees. He entered, then we checked and never saw him exit. I don't know how he did it, but the guy disappeared."

Cody blew out a breath, anger filling him. He didn't want to lose track of this guy. Whoever had shot at Amber needed to go down hard.

After Buckalew arranged for Cody to have access to a computer, he traced the path the man had gone, matching location of cameras on the maps. Buckalew was right, the guy had disappeared. He didn't like admitting defeat.

"I want to go to this park," Cody said when he stepped into Buckalew's office a little while later. "And I want cops to go to each business and get the tapes. We need to find out if there was any more footage of him leaving the park. He had to get out of there somehow, we just have to figure it out."

"How many people do you think we need?" Buckalew asked.

Cody glanced up meeting Cruz's gaze first then Buckalew's. "Let's go with twenty."

"Okay, sounds good," Buckalew said.

"I'll coordinate with you and see how many federal agents we can get. We need to track this guy down."

When they pulled up at the curb near the park, his hope fled. The place was too small, and while there were trees, there weren't enough for someone to stay hidden here for days. This wasn't like Central Park in New York, or Puget Park in Seattle. He could see across the open field of the park with little blocking his view. The one area with trees was small and would be easy to go through.

It took them about twenty minutes to confirm there was no one in the park. Disappointed, he walked around the edge of the park, noticing the lack of street cameras. None of the businesses had cameras with good views of the park either. There were too many blind zones, and areas where the cameras just didn't see the street. That meant the guy knew where to walk to escape detection.

Cody had a suspicion the guy, whoever he was, had to be connected in some way to law enforcement. He hated the thought, but somehow this man knew too much.

* * *

AT FOUR THAT AFTERNOON, Cody found out he was relieved from watching Amber for the evening. Someone else would take the shift, giving him time to relax. He swung by his new apartment complex office and picked up his keys. He felt rushed, though he didn't have to do anything. After checking out his apartment and arranging with the office to open the door for the moving truck driver if he couldn't make it to the apartment when the truck arrived, he found a hotel next to a burger joint and crashed hard, waking close to midnight to find the burger place closed for the night.

He drove over to a Waffle House and ordered the two-egg breakfast. Once he had his water, he pulled up his notes about the case on his phone. It made little sense. Why was Amber being targeted now? The program was almost finished. Maybe the person who wanted her dead didn't know how far along she was. Or they knew and had acted out of anger. Or they were totally random and just enjoyed shooting people.

When his food arrived, he put away his phone and ate, letting his mind wander. He'd been good today, not thinking too much about Amber's curves, or her sexy smile, the way her eyes lit up when she sipped coffee, or how her lips looked perfectly kissable when she was deep in thought, but right now, sitting in this restaurant close to midnight while thoughts of her played through his mind, his cock was hard at the idea of her in bed, snuggled under the covers. He wanted to pull her into his arms and make her see stars.

Shit, he was a pervert and needed to get control of his desire. This was a job, nothing more. Once they figured this out, she would walk away and he'd never see her again.

He stopped chewing and closed his eyes. He didn't want that. Amber wasn't in his life, and she wasn't ever going to be. She was someone the FBI was protecting until they could figure out this case. He needed to remember that. He'd been unlucky in love, losing the one woman who meant the world to him to someone he considered a friend. But then again, he'd been working and his friend had been there when she needed him. Still hurt, but he'd been focused on work and too young— and maybe stupid —to see the writing on the wall.

For him, the FBI wasn't just some random job. He'd become an agent to make a difference. When he'd been in basic training at Parris Island, the men in his bunkhouse had become his brothers. The last week in bootcamp had been shit. They were exhausted and ready to break. Then one of the men, Brandon, had been informed that his little sister had been murdered by gangs on the streets of Boston. It had been difficult to watch Brandon fall apart. The guys had held him up, getting him through the last days, but it had changed Cody. The six years Cody had spent in the Marines had solidified his desire to do more. Every time he'd wanted to give up on the online classes, he'd remembered how heartbroken Brandon's family had been. Sure he'd made a difference overseas as a Marine, but he wanted to make a difference in the States.

The day he graduated the FBI academy and became an agent, he'd emailed Brandon, telling him he would fight to reduce the number of victims like his sister. Brandon had written back, telling him how hard it had been to continue on, but somehow, he'd survived even when he hadn't wanted to. Now Brandon was working for his father in Boston, trying to keep his family from falling apart. News from Brandon had strengthened Cody's resolve to work hard to end organized crime.

He finished his meal and went back to his hotel,

dropping back into bed after replying to a few emails.

His alarm woke him from a dead sleep and he rolled over, groaning at the time. He didn't want to get up, but he had work. Soon he would adjust to the new wakeup time. His furniture would be delivered today, and he wasn't going into the office until after noon unless an emergency popped up. He was just checking his email and responding.

When he got coffee at the local shop, he chuckled as he thought of Amber sipping her first cup when he'd been with her. It was like coffee was a religion for her. If he were heading to see her, he would order another cup.

Why was she taking up space in his mind? She was just someone he'd met on the job, no one special. The lie tasted sour on his tongue. Convincing himself she was nothing wasn't really going to work. He knew there was something special about her.

By some miracle he was at his apartment when his furniture arrived. They'd unloaded everything quickly, not that he had much furniture or that many boxes, but he was amazed they'd finished in less than an hour and had set up his bed.

Before he left for the day, he put clean sheets on

his mattress so when he returned home, he would be able to drop into bed.

His phone rang and he answered, not surprised at all work was calling. "Agent Whittaker here."

"Cody, it's Cruz. Are you heading in soon?"

"Yes, sir. They just finished unloading my furniture."

"Good. Come to the office, we have a lot to go over."

"Sure thing, I'll see you in a few."

He hung up and grabbed his jacket before shutting and locking the door. His phone buzzed and he wondered if Cruz was going to tell him to pick something up on the way, instead it was a text from Amber.

Amber: I was disappointed you weren't on my detail last night.

Cody stared at the text for almost a full minute as he willed his cock to go down. He should tell her he wasn't interested in her.

Cody: Me too.

Oh God, why was he making this worse? The correct response was to blow her off. Tell her he didn't want anything to do with her. That anything she'd seen from him, any interest he'd shown had been because of his job. But he couldn't lie.

Amber: Can you pick me up from work?
Cody: I'll see if I can. I'm headed to the office now.
Amber: Okay. I'll see you later.

Cody shoved his phone into his pocket and let out a growl of frustration. He should step away. He didn't want to use this case as an excuse to get closer to her. He didn't need to see her again to solve this mess. Someone else, a cop, or a different FBI agent could spend time with her, protecting her. He didn't need to be with her to solve anything, but he wanted to see her again, and that made him excited and nervous.

CHAPTER 5

WHEN SHE'D SEEN Cody step into her office, her heart had fluttered with excitement. That excitement hadn't faded as she opened the door to her hotel room and Cody stepped inside behind her, continuing the story from the car.

"Yes, I really did do that," Cody said as he closed the door.

"I can't believe you weren't punished or something."

"Well, they had to find me, and my CO was cool. He wasn't a jerk. He knew he was going to be pranked. I think he liked it."

"So the FBI, not military. What made you change?"

He sighed as sadness crept in on his features. She

could tell he was having an internal war with himself. "I wanted to make a difference."

"Didn't you make a difference as a Marines?"

"Yeah, it's just…"

Amber poured herself a glass of wine and held up an empty glass. "You want any?"

"No thank you. I can't tonight."

"That sucks."

"It's okay. I like my job. I like the difference I make. Moving here, this promotion, it's about increasing the difference, cutting down the number of criminals, making our world safer."

"Do you think you can?" she asked as melancholy drifted over her. She wanted to go home, but the FBI thought it best for her to stay away from her home for a few more days, or until they had a better idea who had tried to kill her.

Cody nodded and sat on the couch. She moved to sit beside him and kicked off her shoes. She pulled her legs up, tucking them underneath her. His gaze traveled over her body and she swore she saw lust in his eyes. He wasn't unaffected by her, just like she wasn't unaffected by him.

Cody swallowed and met her gaze. "I do think I make a difference."

"So tell me the real reason you left the military."

Amber took another sip of wine and turned to face him. She leaned her head on the back of the sofa, positioning herself so she could watch him. His stubble was dark, outlining his jaw. Her fingers itched to touch him.

She desired to taste his mouth and then kiss her way to his ear, finding out if he shivered when she toyed with the lobe. She wanted to seek out all the places that would make him quake from her touch.

Cody cleared his throat and turned to stare straight ahead, his face going blank before he started speaking. "It was the end of basic and we were all exhausted. We'd just come back from our crucible and they pulled one of the guys aside. His little sister had been murdered. His parents weren't sure they would make it to graduation but wanted him to stay. He was caught in a hard place. All of us came together and were his family at that point. We'd been to hell and back, the heat and humidity had done a number on us, and it was an emotional time. I knew being a Marine wasn't something I wanted to do forever, but I made money and had a place to live. When I found out about his sister and learned what happened, my focus changed. Over the next few months I figured out that I wanted to be an FBI agent."

She reached up and cupped his cheek. He turned to face her, and she saw moisture filling his eyes. Her heart went out to him and the only thing she knew to do was lean in and press her lips to his.

The touch was nearly explosive. The impact of his lips could be felt all the way to her toes. At first the kiss was sweet, then she moved, straddling him. The skirt of her dress was loose but still lifted, exposing her thighs to his touch. He ran his hands over her legs then up to her waist as she begged him to open his mouth.

When he finally did open, she was consumed with desire, filled with lust and need that didn't seem to be waning. She deepened the kiss, lifting up so she was almost hanging over him, dominating him.

His fingers slid up her thighs almost to her butt cheeks before they curled in and squeezed. Hot lust made her wet and his touch only stoked her fire higher. She wanted to feel all of him, to taste his skin, to lick his body, and to suck him.

She was ready to take this to the bedroom when he put his hands on her upper arm and eased her away from him. They were both breathing hard and his eyes were darker than normal.

Her cheeks flamed hot as rejection sunk in.

"I want you," Cody said.

"Why are you stopping?"

"Because I'm on the clock, and I've never touched another agent or anyone we were protecting."

She stared down at him, her mind sifting over his words. "But you do want me."

"God yes. Ever since I met you, but I can't, not right now."

"After this is over?"

His lips curved up on one side. "I'm all yours."

She moved off him and closed her eyes as she leaned her head against the couch. His fingers found hers and they twisted together.

"I'm sorry. I want to, but I can't dishonor my commitment to protecting you. Your safety comes first, my needs second."

"What about my needs?"

His nostrils flared as he let go his breath. "You need safety first."

"I want you."

He stood quickly, taking a step away from the couch before turning to face her. "My lust can't eclipse my duty. I like you, Amber Millner. I want to do more than just kiss you, but I can't let you down by having sex while I'm supposed to be protecting you. I would be distracted more than I already am.

But I can promise you this, once we resolve this, I want to see where our desire leads us."

Amber stood and wiped her hand over her dress, smoothing down the skirt. She was about four inches shorter than him without her shoes on and had to stare up at him. Her gaze traced over his stubbled jaw to his thinned lips and finally to his eyes flashing with passion. She shivered as lust pumped hard through her. She noticed the way the stress lines around his eyes softened the longer she held his gaze.

"You're right. I don't want to put you in a difficult position. Yes, I want to have sex with you, but I don't want you to lose your job." She reached out and he took her hand. Their fingers twined together and she lifted his hand to her mouth, kissing the back of it.

This man made her feel differently than any other man she'd ever known. She wanted more than just a one-night stand with him. Maybe if everything worked out, she'd get to see how far they could go.

"I'm going to sleep," Amber said.

"There will be a San Antonio police officer outside your room if you need something. No one should be able to get in here."

"Can you stay?"

He glanced down to his feet and she saw the war inside play out on his face. When he looked up, the passion and light she'd seen earlier was gone. He gave a sharp nod. She should have felt relief, but really all she felt was disappointment that the funny, sexy, amazing man she'd gotten to know over the last few hours was shuttered to her. This was the FBI Agent who would keep her safe but share nothing of his life with her.

Six days had passed since the shooting and Cody was unhappy that they hadn't found any more leads. Amber was going home to her condo which made him nervous. He'd stayed away for two days, working the case on his end, trying not to think about her. They were getting closer mainly based on eliminating suspects, but they weren't close enough.

After work, he headed home and took a shower, washing away the grime from the day. He wanted to talk to Amber, but there wasn't a reason to call her. He'd been serious about not doing anything to jeopardize this case.

He tugged on a pair of gym shorts, skipping the underwear and grabbed his phone, checking the messages as he walked into his kitchen. There was a message from Amber. His lips twitched up at the photo she'd sent. She was holding a bottle of wine and two glasses. He texted back a photo of his car keys.

She sent a photo with her smiling, her thumps up. She looked so happy and inviting. No was the right answer to her request for him to come over for a drink, but he ignored his inner critic and changed into different shorts and a t-shirt before he grabbed his keys and wallet.

The drive to her place took about fifteen minutes with the traffic and when he knocked at her door, his stomach did a double flip. He shouldn't be here. He should walk back to the elevator, get on, and then drive home, but he didn't move.

She pulled open the door and he froze. Her hair was pulled up on top of her head, just waiting for him to free it. She had on a blue t-shirt and dark blue shorts. Her long legs were bare which sent desire rocking through him. His gaze flew to hers and he felt panic rising.

"Don't worry, Agent, I won't bite."

Her words had the opposite reaction than what she'd verbalized. His cock grew impossibly hard as he imagined her licking and nipping her way down his chest to his abs.

"Don't just stand there, get in here," Amber said.

He still said nothing as he stepped inside and moved to the kitchen where the bottle of wine was sitting on the counter. He poured a glass and took a sip.

"You're awfully quiet," Amber said.

"I'm thinking about how crazy I am."

"For what?"

"Coming over here."

"You aren't on the clock. Aren't you allowed to have a personal life?"

"Yes, but that doesn't mean I'm allowed to do things with someone the FBI is providing protection for."

She lifted one eyebrow and leaned in. "Things?"

He cleared his throat trying to push down the runaway desire. "Yes, things."

"What kind of things do you want to do with me?"

He coughed and sputtered though he hadn't drunk anymore wine. "Oh no, we're not talking about that. We can literally talk about anything else, but not what I want to do with you."

Her laughter made his balls pull up tight. He clenched his fist, trying to calm his libido.

"I like you, Cody. There is no question about that. I want to spend time with you, getting to know you."

He nodded and took a sip of the wine. "We can get to know each other."

"Just not biblically."

He'd just taken another sip of wine when she said that. Luckily, he was standing in the kitchen and was able to get most of the stuff spewed from his mouth into the sink. He coughed and Amber was there, rubbing circles on his back.

She handed him a towel and he wiped his face and coughed a few more times. He straightened, trying not to be too embarrassed.

"I'm sorry, I didn't mean to make you choke."

He tried to smile though he felt like pulling her into a kiss. "It's okay."

"Want to watch a movie?"

"Sure." He prayed it wasn't a romance that would put ideas into both of their heads.

"Good. We can order pizza?"

"Sounds good to me." He was hungry and pizza wasn't typically a romantic meal.

"You're very amenable."

His lips twitched up in a smile. "I just like spending time with you."

"Good answer." Amber pulled out her phone and

started ordering the pizza. "Is sausage, onion, black olive, and mushroom okay?"

"That sounds great." She'd picked onion, which meant maybe he would get out of here without kissing her. Not that he didn't want to kiss her, he wanted to kiss her too much.

"Cool." She clicked through a few more screens then set her phone down. "It will take about thirty minutes."

He nodded, thinking he could behave himself for thirty minutes. They picked an action flick which she seemed to enjoy. He was thankful for the fast-paced action with no romance.

The buzzer sounded and he hopped up to grab the pizza. Amber had paused the movie and moved close; her eyes gleaming with excitement.

"I'm so hungry," she said.

He chuckled, his heart feeling lighter. Hanging out with her was fun. They chowed down on pizza while they watched the movie. He was impressed, Amber could put away pizza and didn't apologize for taking a fourth piece.

At the end of the movie, he stood, wishing he could stay longer. She reached out and took his hand, sending a tingling sensation up his arm to his neck that spread over his body.

"I know we can't do...um." Amber's eyes filled with emotions. "I like hanging out with you. This was nice."

He cupped her cheek, rubbing his thumb over her soft skin. "Once things calm down."

"Are you close to catching someone?"

He couldn't tell her. Not because he didn't trust her, but information was compartmentalized at this stage.

"I can't talk about the operation, but I can tell you that it won't go on forever."

She rolled her eyes and placed one hand on his chest, stealing his breath away. His cock lengthened and his balls tightened. He had to be careful or he'd end up in her bed and possibly compromise everything.

He took a step back and saw the disappointment flash in her eyes though she covered it quickly.

"Sorry, I can't—"

Amber's smile tightened as she wrapped her arms around her waist and took a step back. "I understand. You can't throw away your job, but that doesn't mean I don't want you."

He blew out a breath as his desire ramped up. "I want you too."

"So tell me, badass FBI agent who follows the rules, when this is over, will you go out with me?"

He chuckled, thinking her description of him gave him too much credit. "You bet."

"Good." Her lips curved up into a huge smile. "Now be a good boy and go home."

He wanted to pull Amber into a kiss, but that was the opposite of what he should do. He stepped back, ignoring the lust pumping through him. "Okay, lock up and stay safe."

"I will. And that program should be finished by the end of next week. We'll be sending it over to Homeland Security on that Friday, so I'll only have it for a little more than a week and then I'm done with that project."

"That's good." His heart skipped a beat and worry filled him. He prayed that didn't set off the guy. They didn't have long to figure out who held such a huge grudge against Amber. If this guy knew the project was almost complete, he could strike hard, and that was the last thing they needed.

CHAPTER 7

AMBER HADN'T LIKED the worry she'd seen on Cody's face last night. Her gut twisted with apprehension as she made her way into work. She still wasn't driving since she hadn't replaced her car, instead a police office or someone from the FBI drove her to work and picked her up. She was just thrilled they'd determined her home was safe and she could happily return.

She only had a few more days to get everything perfect with the program. She was close, just one more tweak and a few test runs in a beta environment and then she would feel like she'd accomplished everything she'd set out to do.

Mitch stepped into her office, a wide smile on his

face. "Hey, I was wondering if you were ready with the program."

"Almost. I'm finishing it up."

"That's great. So after you turn this in, there are a few projects that need some attention, but I think you should take some time and relax."

She chuckled. "I'm not sure I know how to do that."

"So what about Mexico or Key West? You could go soak up some sun."

The idea of taking a vacation was foreign to her. How long had it been? Four years or more. A heavy sigh fell from her lips.

"I don't know," she said.

"Well, I do. Book a vacation. Go somewhere fun, or do a bunch of spa treatments here, but once you turn this in, you aren't to come back to the office for a week."

She wasn't sure if he was serious, but then his lips thinned. He was kicking her out for a week.

"Okay, I get it. I'll take a week off." She knew she needed the time and wanted to get away, but the reality of traveling alone didn't excite her.

"Good. And don't just sit around here, go do something fun."

Fun. What she'd like to do was spend the week in

Cody's bed, but that would only happen if the FBI solved this case.

After lunch she sent a text to Cody asking if he wanted to meet for dinner. It took almost an hour for him to reply that he would like that. They were getting along well. Maybe taking things slowly was good for them. They could get to know each other without the pressure of sex.

He said he would pick her up from her office at six, which gave her plenty of time to finish her work. She felt good about the changes she'd made in the code and knew on Monday she'd be able to run the final tests they needed to sign off on the project by Tuesday or Wednesday at the latest.

Cody was on time and they headed to a Mexican food place not too far from her condo. The night air had a slight chill and felt good after so many long and hot days. They were seated inside the restaurant at the back where Cody could keep an eye on the door.

"Mitch, my boss, wants me to take a vacation."

"Really?" Cody asked.

"Yep. He thinks I need some time away from the office. I mean I understand his reasonings, but I like work."

"I'm sure you do, but he's probably right."

Chips and salsa were placed on the table along with two glasses of ice water. "I know, but I can't imagine going somewhere mainly because I'd be alone. I guess that's why I haven't taken a vacation."

"So no girl trips for you?"

"Uh, no. I moved here for work and most of my college friends are in other cities. We'd talked about doing trips, but we were all poor and then two of them got married and all of them have kids now and I don't."

"Do you want kids?"

She shrugged and took a bite of chip, dripping salsa on the table in front of her. "Maybe. It's not a burning desire." She wiped up the salsa and met Cody's gaze, wondering if talking about kids was wise. "I think if I had the right partner, I'd want to. But it's a lot of work."

The waitress came over and took their order. She asked for enchiladas and Cody ordered fajitas. They both took sips of water then Cody met her gaze and reached across the table. She took his hand, wishing they were even closer. Touching this man felt good.

"Raising kids is tough. I've seen good agents go down because of kids."

She narrowed her gaze, unsure if she understood. "What does that mean?"

"They can't handle the stress. They can get through murder investigations, can handle getting shot at, but add kids in the mix and it's too much. They quit or ask to leave and do something else out of the field. Kids add a layer of complexity to your life. One day, I would like to have kids, but I'd have to plan for it."

"That sounds reasonable."

They were silent for a moment, her deep in thought about what she wanted out of life. She would hit her thirties soon, not that she couldn't have kids once she was in her thirties, but she knew health wise the earlier the better.

Cody started talking about the FBI academy and living so close to Washington DC. The awkward feeling went away, and they spent the next hour chatting about life. She liked talking to him and wanted to get to know more about this intriguing man.

When they pulled up to her condo building, Cody turned off the car and hopped out, racing around to help her out from the passenger side. He tucked her hand between his body and his arm and led her inside.

They were silent on the way up since another resident was in the elevator with them. At her place, Cody opened the door for her, and they stepped in.

The awkwardness was back. This hadn't been a date, but it had been one. She wanted a kiss but knew Cody had work to think about.

His gaze met hers and she could see how he was weighing the options. She cut short his decision-making process and reached up, pulling him down for a brief brush of lips before she stepped back, putting distance between them.

Cody's eyes were dark with lust. "You're playing a dangerous game."

"I know, and I'm sorry. I don't want you to think I'm not interested because I am. I know that's as much as you can do."

Cody blew out a breath and took a step back, so he was plastered against the door. "Not pulling you into my arms is difficult. I want—" Cody groaned.

"What do you want?" Amber asked.

He met her gaze with a wild-eye stare, his lips curled up into a feral grin and she shivered as her desire skyrocketed.

"I want to slide into you and hold you close as I make love to you."

She lifted her hand and fanned herself. "Oh God."

"You gettin' hot?"

His question sizzled over her nerves. She closed her eyes as the heat rose.

"Tell me, Amber, how do you like it?"

Her eyes flashed open and she let her gaze dip lower to the growing bulge in his pants. Her tongue felt too big, like she needed to lick something juicy.

"Do you like it hard and fast or would you want to go slow?" Cody's voice was low and thick, his eyes were dark and his smile wicked.

She swallowed over the lump in her throat and met his eyes again. "I'd take it however you gave it."

Neither of them moved. This was crazy. They both wanted to be locked in each other's embrace, but their situation was impossible. They couldn't move forward, or he would risk everything. She wouldn't put him in that position.

Cody's hand was on the door handle, white knuckling the knob. She watched as he turned the thing. His jaw was hard, his lips tight as he opened the door and stepped into the hall.

"Soon, Amber, very soon. If you don't want this tell me before we start, because once we get the greenlight, I'm going to move on this."

She nodded because her mouth was too full of lust to speak. Cody shut the door and she moved to the locks, turning them before stepping back. She sunk to the floor and leaned against the wall, her hands over her pussy, cupping her mound. It didn't take anything, just a little light pressure and she was pulsing as she imagined Cody sliding into her.

"Jesus, Cody, what in the world have you done to me?" she whispered before she stood and removed her wet panties. The man got to her. Once they came together, it would be molten fire.

CHAPTER 8

CODY SPENT the weekend going over the information on the case and unpacking. He liked his apartment but he wished it was closer to Amber's place, but then again if he was closer to Amber, he would be over there right now.

He was surprised he hadn't jacked off in his car after their date that wasn't a date. By the time he made it home, he was ready to burst and it only took a few strokes to get off.

He didn't want to suffocate her, but by Sunday afternoon when he hadn't heard from her, he sent a text.

Cody: Hey, how are you doing?
Amber: Wishing we were free to have sex.

Cody shivered as lust ripped through him. He made sure the blinds were closed before he sat back against the couch and texted again.

Cody: What would you do to me?

Amber: Maybe tie you to my bed so you couldn't leave.

A bark of laughter escaped his lips.

Cody: So you're planning on kidnapping an FBI Agent.

Amber: Only in the best way possible. Do you want to grab dinner?

Cody: We have to eat out at a restaurant. I can't be alone with you right now. I'm not strong enough.

Amber: Okay, how about we go to a sports bar and watch a game or something? Someone is playing something.

Cody: Sounds good. I'll be over in a few minutes to pick you up.

Amber: I can't wait.

It took him about thirty minutes to brush his teeth, wash his face, make sure he didn't smell and head out to her place. When he knocked on her door, his heart fluttered. He wanted more than the friendship they'd developed and so did Amber. Soon he would be free to have her in his arms and they wouldn't have to go to a bar, instead he could just step into her home and take her up against the door.

The thought made him so hard he had to calm himself. He drew in a deep breath and pushed the desire away. Of course he wouldn't always take her up against the door, but lust had him so twisted up all he could think about was having sex.

Amber opened the door, her smile wide. "You ready?"

"Sure am. Let's go."

He drove them to a wings place where they ordered a beer and an appetizer of chips with salsa at the bar. They planned on hanging out for a couple of hours and agreed they would order wings later.

The game on all the TVs was between Atlanta and the Texans. Of course everyone was rooting for the Texans. Amber didn't seem to care either way, she just liked watching. Said she enjoyed the game play. It was the third quarter by the time they left the bar seating for a table. He'd had two beers at the bar but wasn't feeling them any longer.

They sat across the table from each other and he wished he could hold her hand. His superiors would probably think his actions were reckless. He guessed they were. Since meeting Amber, he'd changed his mind on what was reckless and what was sane. First off, he thought not having her wild red hair twisted around his fingers was absolutely crazy. He wanted to touch her and never let go.

She spent thirty minutes trying to explain some technical stuff about big data manipulation, but it sounded complicated. At the end, she sighed.

"Why the long face?"

"This project has been big. I don't know what my next big project will be. I'm a little afraid of what will come next."

"You're smart."

She shrugged. "I liked working on this because it was hard. It was a challenge to deal with the problem."

"So do you have your next project lined up?"

She shook her head. "Not yet."

"Will you move to a different company?"

She shrugged. "I don't know. Before I met you, I was willing to relocate. There aren't many programmer positions opened here."

He sat forward, worry filling him. "Will you have to move?"

She took his hand, squeezing and sending good vibes up his arm to his chest. He liked touching her, being with her, and he needed more of her in his life.

"I don't think I'll need to move. I've gained some notoriety in the last few weeks in the industry."

He froze as a wave of panic crashed into him. "Wait, what?"

"The information is out. I mean we knew it would be, but people know I've tackled the issue of parsing data and solved it."

Cody pulled his phone out and started texting Cruz and the rest of his team. "Before I hit send, how did this get out? Who knows?"

"Hold on there, Cody. No one knows exactly what I've been working on, just that I had some big data sorting breakthrough. They don't know it was with Homeland. And they don't know what the end goal is. I've also not spoken about how I accomplished the feat, just that I've tackled big data and am happy with the results."

He shook his head and put his phone on the table without sending the text. Their order of wings came out, but his stomach was in knots. He needed to figure this out. Why hadn't they known about this?

"What exactly happened?" he asked.

She blinked at him a few times. "I'd done an interview a few weeks ago about big data manipulation. It was okayed by Homeland Security and my company. I didn't release any specifics, nor did I talk about the goal of my program."

"Shit, didn't you think we needed to know about this?"

"Cody, I forgot about it," she wiped her fingers on her napkin. "Honestly, I had other things on my mind like not being dead and finishing this project."

He closed his eyes and counted backwards from five. When he opened his eyes, he hated the anger he saw in Amber's gaze. "I'm sorry. I just think we should have known this."

"Really it's in an obscure magazine. I don't think many people will see it."

"But the person wanting you dead could be a jealous co-worker, or competition."

She shook her head. "It would be hard for them to figure out where I was located."

"Not really. Just a few bucks. I need to get this information to my team. Let me send the text then we can eat. I'll need to drop you by your place once we're done."

Her lips thinned. "I wish you could stay."

He nodded, thinking that her admission just made his life more difficult. "I'll have to go to the FBI office. I need to see if this could change things."

Amber's brows bunched and her lips turned down in a frown. "I really didn't think about this interview until now."

He reached across the table and took her hand again. "It's okay. We should have found it. And don't worry, we'll figure out who did this and catch them."

Amber nodded before she took a bite of her wings. He could tell she was worried, and so was he. He didn't like information floating around out there about her. Eventually the FBI would shuffle this to a cold case and he'd move on to something else. They had to solve it for him to feel like Amber was safe, and they had to get this closed if he wanted to date her.

Even heading out to get wings was risky. If anyone with the FBI thought he was acting inappropriately, it could be the end of him.

After they finished eating, he dropped Amber at her place, walking her to her door before racing over to the FBI office. She was right, the article that mentioned her was from a small publication with few subscribers. It was doubtful this had gone out to the general public.

A few hours later they had a list of subscribers and were making their way through travel records for each person. There were eight subscribers who lived in Texas but it didn't seem like any of them were in San Antonio when the shooting happened.

"So she wasn't hiding this?" Cruz asked.

"No, she forgot about it. I guess the article came out last week and it wasn't on her mind."

"So how did you find out?"

Cody turned to face Cruz. They were the only two in the office so he felt he could say something. Cody wiped his hand over his face and dropped his head to the chair and blew out a breath as he stared at the ceiling.

"I was at dinner with her."

Cruz leaned in and Cody sat up, his gaze meeting Cruz's. Neither of them said anything for a long moment.

"Have you done more than take her to dinner?" Cruz asked.

"I told her what I wanted to do once this case is over. We kissed a few times, but that's it."

"Well, you're a stronger man than I am. I couldn't keep my hands off Mickey."

"Wait, was Mickey part of a case you were working on?"

Cruz chuckled and stood. "I'll save that story for later. I have a hot woman waiting for me and I aim to please."

Cody stood and stretched. "I'll see you in the morning."

"Sure will. And Cody, you're a good man. Not

getting involved is the smart move. Once everything settles and you can date her on your own terms it will make it easier."

"Thanks, and I'll remember that tonight as I'm drifting off to sleep alone."

Cruz threw back his head and laughed. "You have two hands for a reason, dude. I'll see you later."

He headed home, wishing he was returning to Amber's place. Before he dropped to his bed, he sent a text.

Cody: I miss you.

Amber: I was just sitting here thinking the same thing. Everything okay?

Cody: Yes. We have more information and we'll tackle it tomorrow. Sleep well.

Amber: You too. I'm glad you texted. I like spending time with you.

Cody: Same here. Soon we'll be able to spend more time together.

Amber: I would like that. Good night. I'll talk to you tomorrow.

Cody slept well that night and was at the office early. Amber had texted first thing, asking him to go car shopping with her this weekend. Of course he'd replied that he would go with her. He still had the FBI-issued car and needed to get his own. He wasn't sure what he wanted for his personal vehicle, but it needed to be nondescript. Not that he would take it to crime scenes, but still flashy cars weren't the norm for most agents.

They combed through information on Amber's case as well as information on two other cases. He felt like they were making some progress. At noon, he broke for lunch with Cruz. They were headed back into the office when his phone buzzed. He glanced down seeing a text from Amber. It took him a second to read the text and process the one word she'd sent.

Help!

What did that mean? Cody reached out and grabbed Cruz's arm.

Cruz turned to him, and his eyes narrowed. "Hey, Cody, what's up?"

"Amber texted me just one word, help with an exclamation mark. See." He turned his phone so Cruz could see the screen.

"Shit. Let's head to her work. I'll drive."

Cody followed after Cruz. He didn't want to think the worst but how could he not? Why would Amber text him for help? Wasn't there a police officer at her place of business in addition to the security? They hopped into Cruz's car and the man pointed it in the direction of Amber's office.

It had been a while since he prayed, but he prayed everything was fine with Amber when he got there. Losing her would be a punch to his gut. He needed her to be safe.

CHAPTER 9

AMBER HAD CLOSED her door earlier in the day when she realized she needed to concentrate to do the final reading of her program. She'd been deep into the code, her mind full of technical issues when she'd heard the first loud pop. She sat up, thinking that noise didn't fit. Then she heard it again.

Pop. Pop.

Fear blasted through her and immediately her hands and legs started shaking. Her stomach turned and she kind of wanted to throw up.

The hair on the back of her neck rose. The gunfire was for her.

People she worked with were screaming. Her fear increased. Pounding footsteps raced past her office as people scrambled for the emergency exit.

The alarm was pulled, drowning out some of the noise, but she could still hear the gunfire.

She grabbed her phone and typed in one word, hitting send to Cody. He would know what to do.

Escape was her only goal. Amber slowly opened the door to her office. The sound of the alarm took her breath away. Then she saw him and her hands and knees shook more. The guy had a gun and he looked intent on finding something.

Though panic ruled, she had enough presence of mind to drop to all fours. Air left her lungs in a whoosh. Her muscles shook and panic told her to stay put, but she forced herself to crawl from her office to the supply closet. The exit stairs were an option, but everyone was going that way. The guy would see her since the exit door was located at the end of the long hall. He would follow and find her. The supply closet door was down a hall and opened in a way the man wouldn't be able to see her enter. It was her best option.

Every inch she moved was filled with fear. Every sound she made induced gut churning panic. Finally, she made it to the closet and eased open the door. Though her whole body was shaking like a leaf, she crawled in and then slowly closed the door, trying not to draw any attention to herself.

She made her way to the back corner, fear riding her hard, making it difficult to breathe. She needed to find a way to escape. Anything she put in place to block entry into the supply closet would fail. The racks of shelving were bolted to the floor, the file cabinets were fixed in place too. She had no way to get out.

There was still the exit door. Her mind spun with the possibilities. If she ran down the stairs, she could be outside in minutes. She would be free, but still trapped in the confines of the compound. Even if she made it outside, there was no place to hide. The fence would keep everyone in. Maybe there was a door at the back of the fence, or she could make it to the gate at the front, but she would be exposed.

This man would search for her. The thought that this was just some random shooter came to mind again, but she dismissed it. It was too close to her being shot at for it to be a coincidence.

Amber closed her eyes, trying to think of a plan. If she stayed here, he would eventually find her, but if she left this room and ran for the stairs, he would see her. She was trapped.

The sound of gunfire grew closer and she had to stifle her scream. Then her phone buzzed and she jumped. Thank goodness she'd turned the device to vibrate mode. She feared the noise of the vibration would draw his attention, so she pulled out her phone and switched it to do not disturb mode.

Cody had texted back, asking her what was wrong. She didn't have time to type out a long reply, but he needed to be warned. With shaky fingers, she typed in *Shooter* and hit send.

Her life was screwed up. She wasn't supposed to be attacked like this, not while at work. This happened to other people, not her and not here.

She flipped on her flashlight and glanced up, seeing that the ceiling here wasn't solid. It was a drop-down type of ceiling, which meant she might be able to escape. Hope filled her.

Amber shown the lowest setting of her phone's flashlight on the shelf and ceiling, getting an idea of what she needed to do to climb up. There were six shelves and there was about two feet from the top of the unit to the ceiling. She felt prepared and turned off the flashlight.

With a calming breath, she started her climb, forcing herself to go slow so she didn't make any noise. It was difficult and the shelves weren't as sturdy as she'd assumed they would be.

Once at the top, Amber breathed out a sigh of

relief. She reached up and pushed on the ceiling tile. It came out easily.

Bam! Bam!

Amber jerked, almost falling off the top shelf. Her body was shaking, and she wanted to cry. The gunman had moved closer. Fear held her and she wasn't sure she would survive past the hour. She wanted to escape, and she also wanted to call her family and tell them she loved them but that would make noise. She was torn. She glanced at her phone and saw there was a notification. Cody had texted. She wanted to look, but she couldn't take the time. She lifted up on her knees, wobbling a little as the shelf shifted under her.

Her fingers curled around the metal frame used to hold the ceiling tiles in place. She almost dropped the phone but held on as she used the flashlight to figure out how she could escape.

There wasn't any way the frame used to mount the false ceiling tiles would hold her. It wasn't meant to be weight bearing. She examined the space and saw that the wall about two feet away from her current position didn't go all the way to the ceiling. What was next door?

She thought about the layout of the building. She was in the supply closet which was next to the emergency exit. But this wall of the closet wasn't next to the stairwell, instead it backed up to the offices on the other side of the building. But what was there? She hardly ever went over to that area. They were a part of the same company, but a different division. Maybe it was their supply closet. Was anyone over there shooting up the place? There was only one way to find out. If she stayed here, she would probably die, but maybe she could escape by climbing over the wall and into the other area.

Amber replaced the ceiling tile above her and crawled along the top of the shelf, hating the way the thing wobbled as her body shook. She sucked in a breath and lifted to her knees. The shelf she was on now wobbled even more than the last one and she had to reach up and out to catch herself. Her hand ran into the ceiling tile, popping it out of the frame. It clattered and almost dropped to the ground. She caught it with her right hand as she grabbed onto the frame with her left, slicing her palm open on the sharp edges of the metal.

"Shit," she whispered then panic set in. What if the shooter had heard her? She needed to move fast.

She shoved the bulky tile back into the ceiling so she could move it back into place before she crawled into the other room.

Somehow the siren stopped blaring, instead it was just a little ping every few seconds. That she could deal with.

The wobble of the shelf made her move slower than she wanted. People were still screaming in her office, and that made her want to hurry, but she couldn't rush this or she would fall.

Her fingers shook as she clutched the top of the wall where it was unfinished and pulled herself up. The mornings at the gym and yoga sessions she'd done for years helped, but her knees still shook as she stood. She would be totally screwed if she didn't work out on a regular basis. What if she hadn't spent hours at the gym building her muscles? There would be no way for her to escape.

Once she was perched on the top of the thin wall, she moved into position to replace the ceiling tile. It was tough to balance on the thin ledge while reaching for the tile. Her heart leapt as fear took over when she heard a guy's voice.

"Where are you? Come out, come out, I know you're close."

He sounded like he was right outside the storage closet. Was he about to open the door? The tile was almost back in place when the squeak of the door opening filled the space. Her stomach rolled and she almost fell from her position on the top of the wall. She let go of the edge of the tile and it dropped into place.

The lights flipped on, a little bit leaking through the top of the lights into the crawlspace where she was hiding, allowing her to see more than a few feet in front of her. There was nothing, just ceiling tile frames, lighting, wires, and a few tubes that probably ran to the water sprinklers.

If she moved now, he would hear. Fear held her as she fought to breathe as shallow as possible while she waited for him to leave.

"Fuck," the man's voice filtered up to the ceiling.

She waited for the door to close, but the lights didn't dim and the door didn't shut. She was stuck in this awkward position, pain making her legs cramp. Her arms hurt too and her fingers were digging into the wall as she fought to stay steady.

"I can't find her. You said she'd be here." The guy's voice was strong with no real accent. "Well she isn't. I'm headed out. The cops should be here soon if they aren't already."

Amber wanted to cheer, but if this guy heard one noise from her, she'd be dead. If she hadn't moved when she had, she would be dead. Oh hell, so much had happened, and she'd almost died.

The sound of the door shutting made her want to relax, but what if he'd stayed in the supply closet. She held still though her legs ached and her arms cried out for relief. Then she heard someone yelling.

Amber waited.

Another person was shouting, telling everyone the guy had left. She didn't want to believe it, but she needed to move. Amber reached for the ceiling tile below her on the new side of the wall and lost her balance. She slipped and her knees hit first, busting the tile below her as she fought to hang onto the top of the wall where she'd been crouching. Her fingers dug into the wall, her nails breaking as her feet smacked into a shelf below, shooting pain up her legs.

Fear held her and she waited for a shot to ring out, but nothing happened. With her whole body on edge, she slowly lowered herself, her fingers clutching anything she could grab onto to steady herself. She was on the cabinet then her feet were on the second from the top shelf, and then the third from the top as she climbed down.

Her breath was coming in gasps. Tears and snot were running down her face. She made it to the door, too scared to open it. What if someone was there with a gun? What if she was killed by a cop because she'd opened the door too fast?

Amber pulled out her phone, tears blurring her vision. She'd received multiple texts from Cody and about six calls. She tapped the screen to dial him back.

"Amber, are you okay?" Cody sounded frantic.

"Yes," she wailed through her tears.

"Where are you?"

"I don't know. I-I—oh God. Cody, come find me."

"Okay, just—hold on."

He must have muted the phone because she couldn't hear anything. It seemed like forever before she heard him breathing again. "The SWAT team is entering the building. Just stay put."

"I'm-I'm in a closet." Her voice and hands shook. "I-I climbed over a wall through the ceiling. He was looking for me."

"Are you sure?" Cody's voice was strained.

"Yes, I heard him. I heard him, Cody."

"Give me a minute."

Cody put his phone on mute again and went over to the operations commander. "I know why this guy was here."

"What? Who are you?"

"I'm FBI Agent Cody Whittaker. There was a

woman targeted here the other night. This shooter wanted her."

"Is she safe?" the cop asked.

"Yes, sir. I'm on the phone with her."

"Give me your phone."

"Okay, let me tell her—" The cop held out his hand. Cody took the phone off mute and spoke. "The operations commander from the police is going to speak to you."

"Oh God, Cody, come get me." He sucked in a breath and handed the phone to the commander.

"Hello, this is Captain Delgany, I'm with the San Antonio police department. Are you okay, have you been shot?"

Cody held his breath as he waited for Delgany to say something.

"Well that's good. So where are you?" Delgany asked.

The relief he felt wouldn't be more than a tiny sliver until he saw Amber with his own eyes. He should have been here, but they had a cop here and how were they to know this man would act today?

Delgany handed him back his phone. "Amber, are you there?"

"Yes, the cop said a couple of guys would make their way up to me. I'm scared."

Cody hated the fear in her voice, but she was alive. She'd survived. "I'll stay on the line with you."

"Thank you."

Cody moved away from the command post, watching the building as he stayed on the line with Amber. "So you weren't hurt?"

"I wasn't shot. I cut my hand and I probably have other scratches. Honestly, I'm so hyped up I don't know what all is wrong."

He looked around, seeing four ambulances in the lot. "EMTs are here and if they're busy, I'll get you to a hospital to get treated."

Delgany stepped close. "We are letting in a couple of your guys. Do you have an FBI vest?"

"Hold on, Amber." He put the phone on mute and turned to Delgany. "I do."

"Well, go get it and you can go in with your team. Cruz is leading it."

Cody turned and saw Cruz holding out a flack vest and a shirt with FBI emblazoned on the front and back.

"Thank you." Cody unmuted his phone. "Amber, I'm not hanging up on you, but I'm going to have to mute you for a moment."

"What's going on? Please tell me the guy isn't here still."

He hated the fear in her voice, and he didn't know where the guy was. They had no clue. He decided not to say anything because it might be a lie. "I'm coming in to get you. I need to put on a vest."

"Oh thank God," Amber breathed out.

"Just hang tight where you are and I'll be there."

"I don't know where I am. I went into the supply closet near my office and ended up over the wall in another closet."

"Okay, don't hang up. And whatever you do, don't jump out. If one of the SWAT team members gets there before me, just keep your hands up and don't make any fast moves."

"You're scaring me." Her voice shook even more.

"Be safe. That's all I'm saying. The SWAT guys are there to help."

He checked his Glock and ammunition before he grabbed the tactical vest from Cruz along with a shirt with large "FBI" printed on the back and front in block letters. He pulled on the vest and then the shirt as he moved to stand beside other FBI officers, all dressed like he was.

Cruz was positioned by a table with a drawing of the building laid out. "The person we're looking for is on the fourth floor, but we don't know exactly where."

"Actually," Cody interrupted him. "I think I know exactly where she is."

Cruz blinked at him. "When were you planning on divulging?"

"Sorry." Cody moved closer to the table. He stared at the drawing of the building. It took him about five seconds to find the supply closet. "She crawled over the wall in this closet. She's in the room here." Cody pointed to what looked to be another supply closet.

"Okay," Cruz nodded as he moved away from the table. "We're headed to the storage closet, fourth floor."

"We're coming up to get you," Cody said after he took the phone off mute.

"You need to take elevators to the right," Amber said.

"She said elevators to the right," Cody relayed.

Cruz acknowledged his words and led the team to the stairwell on the right and entered the override code. They made their way up, using safety procedures to make sure they weren't caught unaware by the guy who'd come in with guns blazing.

They entered the fourth floor, moving slowly, clearing each office. It took another ten minutes to enter every office, check under every desk, in every closet and bathroom. They hadn't found Amber. Worry filled him. What if they were in the wrong area?

A drop of sweat slid down the side of his face and he lifted his shoulder, wiping off the moisture on his shirt. The mission was almost done, but there was still so much they had to accomplish, mainly rescuing Amber and getting her out of here.

Cruz approached a door and pulled it open. He heard Amber's voice.

"Don't shoot. It's me," Amber cried out.

Cody breathed out a sigh of relief. He moved to the closet door and stepped in, his hands shaking as he saw the woman he wanted to make his sitting on the floor looking so afraid he just wanted to hold her close and never let her go. "Amber."

She blinked up at him, tears streaming down her cheeks. He knelt in front of her, searching her face. There was blood smeared on her forehead and nose, but he didn't see any big cuts on her head. She did have a few scratches on her face and dust in her hair, but she didn't look too bad.

"Let's get you up. Can you stand?"

She nodded and pushed herself up, but her legs were still shaking. She drew in a ragged breath, unsure if she could actually walk out on her own.

Cody put his arm around her and pulled her close. She went without hesitation. His hands on her body felt good, reassuring.

They stepped out from the closet and she blinked against the bright light streaming in from the windows. She'd been in the dark for so long, she'd forgotten it was daytime. For some reason she thought it would be night when they came out. Maybe it hadn't been that long, but it had felt like forever up on the ledge, holding on for dear life so some idiot didn't shoot her.

She drew in a deep breath, trying to catch the scent of Cody's aftershave or his shampoo, anything to take away the dusty smell that clogged her nose, reminding her of hiding in the ceiling, just waiting for the jerk to kill her.

A door banged open behind them and she froze. Cody turned, loosening his hold on her. Then she turned too, spinning to see a guy with a gun. Someone shouted just before Cody shoved her behind his body.

She watched over his shoulder in horror as the guy lifted his gun, pointing it at Cody.

Bam!

She screamed and covered her ears as her knees gave out. Then she felt Cody's hands on her, pulling her up. She tried to look back, but Cody kept her facing the other way.

"Don't look, babe. It's taken care of."

She sputtered something, but it wasn't words. Cody helped her down the stairs to the exit where she was met by paramedics. The day's events had freaked her out. She wanted to cry and she wanted to hit something.

Cody stayed with her as she was loaded onto a gurney, and he only stepped away to chat with Cruz for a moment. The fear she'd felt in the ceiling while she'd been holding on for dear life came back.

The thump of the backdoors shutting made her jump. She jerked her head up, searching for Cody, finding him right beside her.

"Is he dead?" Amber asked.

Cody nodded. "Yes, he's gone."

"What about other people at work? Did anyone..." She swallowed over the lump in her throat.

Cody shook his head. "The guy wasn't shooting to kill others. He did hit one guy in the arm, otherwise he was just shooting wide, not really trying to kill anyone. His only target was you."

She nodded, worry filling her. "Any idea who he worked for?"

"Cruz is working on some leads. I'll need to get on the phone once we get you to the hospital."

She closed her eyes and blew out a breath. They needed to find the person or group responsible for trying to kill her. Her program was set to be delivered to Homeland Security at the end of the week. She didn't know what the person would accomplish by killing her now. It wasn't like anyone could stop the roll out since the program was finished.

Maybe they didn't understand how computer programs worked. She thought it had to be some fringe group that didn't have a clue, but it could be a government employee too. She was just relieved Cody had been there to save her.

If she'd left that closet before Cody had arrived, the guy would have killed her. Having Cody and Cruz and the rest of the FBI men protecting her had saved her.

She held onto Cody's hand when they wheeled her into the ER. He kissed her forehead before he turned to leave. Her heart squeezed as he headed out. It was time to move their relationship forward. She didn't want to be apart any longer, she just wanted Cody by her side and in her life all the time.

CHAPTER 10

CODY PULLED OUT HIS PHONE, checking the messages Cruz had sent. They'd found the guy's apartment outside of San Antonio, almost in New Braunfels. They had a team over there, searching through his stuff. The media had picked up on that part of their investigation but hadn't keyed into the fact Amber was involved.

Cody called Cruz when he stepped out of the hospital. "Hey, Cody, how is she?"

"She'll be okay. Do we have any affiliation, any clue who he is working for?"

"No, nothing yet."

"So anyone could be coming after her."

"Maybe. We don't know."

Cody didn't move far away from the door,

knowing she was safe inside for now, but what he didn't know was if there was someone who would come here looking for her.

"We need protection on her."

"I'll order something," Cruz said.

"I hate this."

"Me too. We'll keep her safe. I know how you feel."

He met Cruz's gaze and saw the compassion mixed in with the seriousness. No question, Cruz knew he had fallen for Amber. He'd fought hard not to get involved, but his heart had a mind of its own where she was concerned.

"I tried to hide it."

Cruz chuckled. "It's impossible when they get to you. I know I couldn't hide it with Mickey."

"I can't anymore with Amber." He scanned the parking lot as he spoke, searching for anything off. "I'm going back in. Once someone shows up to guard her, I'll go where you need me."

"Sure thing. Talk to you later."

Cody hung up and moved to go inside, but the hairs on his arm stood on end. He stopped and turned, his nerves on high alert. What had changed?

Again he looked out into the lot, but this time he studied the cars, looking for something different. On the third row he spotted it. A blue truck with a camper on top. It looked out of place mixed with the sedans and other trucks in the lot. Was it the camper or something else? Cody stepped inside, moving quickly to the area where Amber was. A nurse was with her, and nothing seemed amiss.

Cody left the room and walked outside again, his focus on the blue truck. He was about to walk out to the truck and take a closer look when a guy stepped out of the camper. The man had a heavy jacket on which seemed too much for the heat of the day.

Then the jacket moved away from the guy's body as he turned and Cody spied the flash of a gun. He ducked behind a pillar and pulled out his phone. He sent a quick text to Cruz, *shooter at hospital*, and then dialed for backup. The local police would be able to make it to the scene first. He wished he could call the FBI SWAT in for back up, but it would take too long for them to arrive since they were scattered across the city and not just sitting around waiting for a call.

Cody told the woman who answered the phone what was going down and she said a team would be dispatched. Then he called the hospital and asked for an immediate lockdown. He glanced around the edge of the brown brick column he was hiding behind and saw that the guy had made it to the first row of cars. Cody would have to stop him before he got inside.

With a deep breath, he stepped out and lifted his gun. "FBI stop and raise your hands," Cody shouted.

The guy didn't stop. Instead he reached for his gun. Cody had a second to make a decision. He couldn't wait for this man to have his gun out.

Birds flew and he heard someone inside scream when he pulled the trigger. He'd aimed for the leg and watched as the guy dropped to the ground.

Cody wasn't in the clear. The man was in pain, on the ground, but he still had his gun.

Cody inched forward, his gaze staying on the guy, making sure he didn't reach for his weapon. All the training in the world didn't take away the tightness in his stomach as he approached the man.

Sirens came closer and Cody pulled out his phone, hitting redial. When the line was answered he didn't wait for the person to talk.

"This is Agent Cody Whittaker. Your men just pulled into the lot, tell them not to shoot me. I have one down."

He shoved his phone back into his pants, fighting to keep his focus on the man on the ground as he grabbed his FBI credentials and flashed them at the police officers getting out of their cars.

"FBI, don't shoot."

"Okay, man, just stay calm," a cop said as he approached.

"He's got a gun on his right side," Cody said.

Another cop moved in close and disarmed the man Cody had shot. Then the guy was cuffed and Cody blew out a breath in relief.

"Thank God you guys showed up," Cody said.

"What's his deal?" the cop asked.

"Let's get him into the ER and I'll tell you." His phone rang and he pulled it out, seeing it was Cruz. "Hey, we have the evidence."

"Great," Cody said. "I just shot a guy."

"Okay, you first. Is Amber okay?" Cruz asked.

"She is. The guy never made it into the hospital. I saw his gun, I told him I was FBI and asked him to stop. He reached for his gun and I shot him in the leg."

"So he's still alive?" Cruz asked.

"Yes."

"Good, because we have names, dates for meetings, and people. They caught wind of the program and thought if they could stop Amber, the program wouldn't go live. They weren't very organized. I'm actually surprised they pulled off everything they did. If they'd had just a little more planning and a few more people who were good at this sort of thing, she would have been dead weeks ago."

Cruz's words hit him in the chest and he had to suck in air to stay standing. "Shit."

"Yep. But now we know about them. Looks like we can get them on other charges too."

"Good." Cody watched as the guy was loaded onto a gurney and cuffed to the bars. "Hold on." Cody moved closer to the cops. "What's his name?"

"Stewart Birsansky."

"Did you hear that?" Cody asked.

"Sure did, and he's on the list," Cruz said.

"How many more?"

"Four. Go be with Amber, we'll shut them down on our end."

Cody blew out a breath in relief. "Okay, and Cruz, thank you."

"No problem. All in a day's work."

Cody chuckled as he hung up. He headed into the hospital and found Amber. She reached for him and he took her hand, vowing to never let her go.

"Looks like Miss Millner can go," the nurse said when she stepped in.

"Thank you," Amber said as she sat up.

"You'll probably be tired, so take it easy."

"She will," Cody said as he helped Amber to standing.

The cops had Birsansky and there wasn't much for him to do. He led Amber out to his car and helped her strap in. She had cuts on both hands, but only one was bad enough to require stitches.

"I guess I should go home," Amber said.

"I think the location of your home needs to change," Cody met her gaze and held it.

"Really, why?"

"Because I want to live with you."

Amber's lips twitched up. Her green eyes were tired, but they shone with happiness. "You should move in with me."

"Your place is small, maybe we should get a new place, something between both of our offices."

"I'd like that, but I'm not sure I'm going to stay working there."

"Too many memories?" Cody asked.

She shivered then placed her hand on Cody's leg as he drove to her place. "Too many bad ones. I want to move forward and concentrate on the good."

"Same here."

"You're a good man, Cody Whittaker."

"And you're a good woman."

Warmth filled him as he drove. He wouldn't let

Amber get away. She was his, and now he was free to make sure she knew exactly how he felt.

He pulled into the lot of her building and shut off the car. He unbuckled and leaned in close to her, his lips sliding over hers. He shivered as excitement filled him. He would spend the rest of his life making sure this woman knew how special she was.

"I want to spend the night in your arms," Amber whispered.

"Trust me, love, you'll never be without me again."

His lips covered hers and he delved in for a deep kiss, thanking his lucky stars he'd moved to Texas and found this beautiful woman who rocked his world like he rocked hers.

They made their way upstairs where he carefully undressed her then shucked his clothes before stepping into the shower with her. She couldn't get her hand wet, so he had to wash her body for her. His fingers ran over her shoulders and down to her breasts. He loved touching her like this. He covered them with his hands then squeezed her nipples. She moaned as she let her head drop back.

Cody lowered his head and sucked in one nipple then the other, all the while thinking he was the luckiest man in the world. The fingers of her good hand were in his hair as he kissed lower.

Cody was on his knees, his lips on her belly as he drew in a deep breath. He needed Amber. Then he traced a path lower and swiped his tongue over her folds. She spread her legs and he pushed his tongue into her slit, finding her clit in no time. He sucked on the bud, taking her desire higher. She cried out as he sucked harder then went back to just licking.

He couldn't hold back, but he didn't have a condom. He stood and settled for rubbing the tip of his dick over her opening before teasing her clit with the flat head.

"Please, Cody, take me," Amber begged.

"I don't have a condom."

"I don't care. I want you. God, I need you."

The urge to take her grew, but he wouldn't. Instead he used his fingers to slide into her wet heat. It felt amazing and he couldn't wait to have his dick buried deep inside her. She was magnificent, a beauty to behold.

It only took a few times pumping in while he brushed his thumb over her clit before she came, riding out her orgasm. Amber threw back her head and shouted his name as she came. Her hand held his in place as she pulsed around his fingers, making him harder.

When she let go of his hand, he fisted is cock and jerked himself off. His orgasm grew stronger and he tugged her close, using the friction of rubbing his cock up against her belly to finish off. His seed spilled between them and heated his stomach.

Amber looked up, her lips parted and her eyes full of emotions. He cupped her cheek and brushed a gentle kiss over her lips.

"I promise to be there for you," he whispered.

"And I promise to always hold you close." Amber pulled him down into another kiss, making his heart sing.

He'd found a home with this woman. She was all the things he needed from love to comfort and more. They were made for each other; he had no doubt. Already his heart was full of love for her, and he could see love shining back at him.

Cody stared into her eyes, his heart fuller than ever as he whispered, "Forever, Amber, I promise to give you forever."

The End

ABOUT THE AUTHOR

Julia Bright is the author of the contemporary military romance Dark Eagle series and is an Operation Alpha Author. Julia lives in the south where "bless your heart" is an insult and "shut up" shows love. Julia has been reading since they could open a book and has taken the passion for words and combined it with the love of travel to create stories full of passion and excitement. If you love a good book with a fantastic happily ever after, you'll enjoy a Julia Bright novel. For a dash of paranormal romance and urban fantasy, pick up a book from Julia's USA Today Bestselling JS Bright pen name

Special Forces: Operation Alpha

Saving Lorelei

Rescuing Amy

Saving Sloan

Justice for Amber

Dark Eagle Series

Survive The Fall

Live Past The Edge

Standalone Romance

Acting The Part

All Business

Just One Taste

There are many more books in this fan fiction world than listed here, for an up-to-date list go to www.AcesPress.com

You can also visit our Amazon page at:
http://www.amazon.com/author/operationalpha

Special Forces: Operation Alpha World
Denise Agnew: Dangerous to Hold
Shauna Allen: Awakening Aubrey
Shauna Allen: Defending Danielle
Shauna Allen: Rescuing Rebekah
Shauna Allen: Saving Scarlett
Shauna Allen: Saving Grace
Brynne Asher: Blackburn
Jennifer Becker: Hiding Catherine
Julia Bright: Saving Lorelei
Julia Bright: Rescuing Amy
Victoria Bright: Surviving Savage
Victoria Bright: Going Ghost
Victoria Bright: Jostling Joker
Cara Carnes: Protecting Mari
Kendra Mei Chailyn: Beast
Kendra Mei Chailyn: Barbie
Kendra Mei Chailyn : Pitbull
Melissa Kay Clarke: Rescuing Annabeth

Melissa Kay Clarke: Safeguarding Miley
Samantha A. Cole: Handling Haven
Samantha A. Cole: Cheating the Devil
Sue Coletta: Hacked
Melissa Combs: Gallant
KaLyn Cooper: Rescuing Melina
Liz Crowe: Marking Mariah
Jordan Dane: Redemption for Avery
Jordan Dane: Fiona's Salvation
Riley Edwards: Protecting Olivia
Riley Edwards: Redeeming Violet
Riley Edwards, Recovering Ivy
Nicole Flockton: Protecting Maria
Nicole Flockton: Guarding Erin
Nicole Flockton: Guarding Suzie
Nicole Flockton: Guarding Brielle
Casey Hagen: Shielding Nebraska
Casey Hagen: Shielding Harlow
Casey Hagen: Shielding Josie
Casey Hagen: Shielding Blair
Desiree Holt: Protecting Maddie
Kathy Ivan: Saving Sarah
Kathy Ivan: Saving Savannah
Kathy Ivan: Saving Stephanie
Jesse Jacobson: Protecting Honor
Jesse Jacobson: Fighting for Honor

Jesse Jacobson: Defending Honor

Jesse Jacobson: Summer Breeze

Silver James: Rescue Moon

Silver James: SEAL Moon

Silver James: Assassin's Moon

Silver James: Under the Assassin's Moon

Becca Jameson: Saving Sofia

Kate Kinsley: Protecting Ava

Heather Long: Securing Arizona

Heather Long: Guarding Gertrude

Heather Long: Protecting Pilar

Heather Long: Covering Coco

Gennita Low: No Protection

Kirsten Lynn: Joining Forces for Jesse

Margaret Madigan: Bang for the Buck

Margaret Madigan: Buck the System

Margaret Madigan: Jungle Buck

Margaret Madigan: December Chill

Rachel McNeely: The SEAL's Surprise Baby

Rachel McNeely: The SEAL's Surprise Bride

Rachel McNeely: The SEAL's Surprise Twin

KD Michaels: Saving Laura

KD Michaels: Protecting Shane

KD Michaels: Avenging Angels

Wren Michaels: The Fox & The Hound

Wren Michaels: The Fox & The Hound 2

Wren Michaels: Shadow of Doubt

Wren Michaels: Shift of Fate

Wren Michaels: Steeling His Heart

Kat Mizera: Protecting Bobbi

Mary B Moore: Force Protection

LeTeisha Newton: Protecting Butterfly

LeTeisha Newton: Protecting Goddess

LeTeisha Newton: Protecting Vixen

LeTeisha Newton: Protecting Heartbeat

MJ Nightingale: Protecting Beauty

MJ Nightingale: Betting on Benny

MJ Nightingale: Protecting Secrets

Sarah O'Rourke: Saving Liberty

Debra Parmley: Protecting Pippa

Lainey Reese: Protecting New York

Jenika Snow: Protecting Lily

Jen Talty: Burning Desire

Jen Talty: Burning Kiss

Jen Talty: Burning Skies

Jen Talty: Burning Lies

Jen Talty: Burning Heart

Megan Vernon: Protecting Us

Megan Vernon: Protecting Earth

Police and Fire: Operation Alpha World

Freya Barker: Burning for Autumn

KaLyn Cooper: Justice for Gwen
Aspen Drake: Sheltering Emma
Deanndra Hall: Shelter for Sharla
Deanndra Hall: Justice for Aleta
Barb Han: Kace
Reina Torres: Justice for Sloane
Stacey Wilk: Stage Fright

As you know, this book included at least one character from Susan Stoker's books. To check out more, see below.

SEAL of Protection: Legacy Series

Securing Caite

Securing Brenae (novella)

Securing Sidney

Securing Piper (Aug 2019)

Securing Zoey (Jan 2020)

Securing Avery (May 2020)

Securing Kalee (Sept 2020)

Delta Force Heroes Series

Rescuing Rayne (FREE!)

Rescuing Aimee (Novella)

Rescuing Emily

Rescuing Harley

Marrying Emily (novella)

Rescuing Kassie

Rescuing Bryn

Rescuing Casey

Rescuing Sadie (novella)

Rescuing Wendy

Rescuing Mary

Rescuing Macie (novella)

Badge of Honor: Texas Heroes Series

Justice for Mackenzie (FREE!)

Justice for Mickie

Justice for Corrie

Justice for Laine (novella)

Shelter for Elizabeth

Justice for Boone

Shelter for Adeline

Shelter for Sophie

Justice for Erin

Justice for Milena

Shelter for Blythe

Justice for Hope

Shelter for Quinn

Shelter for Koren (July 2019)

Shelter for Penelope (Oct 2019)

SEAL of Protection Series

Protecting Caroline (FREE!)

Protecting Alabama

Protecting Fiona

Marrying Caroline (novella)

Protecting Summer

Protecting Cheyenne

Protecting Jessyka
Protecting Julie (novella)
Protecting Melody
Protecting the Future
Protecting Kiera (novella)
Protecting Alabama's Kids (novella)
Protecting Dakota

New York Times, USA Today and *Wall Street Journal* Bestselling Author Susan Stoker has a heart as big as the state of Tennessee where she lives, but this all American girl has also spent the last fourteen years living in Missouri, California, Colorado, Indiana, and Texas. She's married to a retired Army man who now gets to follow *her* around the country.

She debuted her first series in 2014 and quickly followed that up with the SEAL of Protection Series, which solidified her love of writing and creating stories readers can get lost in.

If you enjoyed this book, or any book, please consider leaving a review. It's appreciated by authors more than you'll know.

www.stokeraces.com
www.AcesPress.com
susan@stokeraces.com

Made in the USA
Columbia, SC
17 April 2023